"Don't do it for me. Do it for the kids,"
Garrett insisted.

Darby looked up at him. She'd told him to put the children's welfare first. Could she do anything less?

She could handle a week, couldn't she? She wouldn't be foolish enough to lose her heart again to children who wouldn't be hers. She certainly wouldn't lose her heart to this man. "Would you need someone from say, nine to five?" she asked rather desperately.

"Around the clock," Garrett said smoothly.

"I can't…live with you."

"Why not? My business keeps me busy enough that I'm hardly around anyway."

"Garrett, if you don't plan to love those kids, why are you so determined to keep them?"

He was silent for a moment. "Because I promised my sister that I would not fail her. Help me not fail her kids."

Dear Reader,

The most wonderful time of the year just got better! These six captivating romances from Special Edition are sure to brighten your holidays.

Reader favorite Sherryl Woods is back by popular demand with the latest addition to her series AND BABY MAKES THREE: THE DELACOURTS OF TEXAS. In *The Delacourt Scandal*, a curious reporter seeking revenge unexpectedly finds love.

And just in time for the holidays, Lisa Jackson kicks off her exciting new miniseries THE McCAFFERTYS with *The McCaffertys: Thorne,* where a hero's investigation takes an interesting turn when he finds himself face-to-face with his ex-lover. Unwrap the next book in A RANCHING FAMILY, a special gift this month from Victoria Pade. In *The Cowboy's Gift-Wrapped Bride,* a Wyoming rancher is startled not only by his undeniable attraction to an amnesiac beauty he found in a blizzard, but also by the tantalizing secrets she reveals as she regains her memory.

And in RUMOR HAS IT…, a couple separated by tragedy in the past finally has a chance for love in Penny Richards's compelling romance, *Lara's Lover.* The holiday cheer continues with Allison Leigh's emotional tale of a runaway American heiress who becomes a *Mother in a Moment* after she agrees to be nanny to a passel of tots.

And silver wedding bells are ringing as Nikki Benjamin wraps up the HERE COME THE BRIDES series with the heartwarming story of a hometown hero who convinces his childhood sweetheart to become his *Expectant Bride-To-Be.*

I hope all of these breathtaking romances warm your hearts and add joy to your holiday season.

Best,
Karen Taylor Richman
Senior Editor

Please address questions and book requests to:
Silhouette Reader Service
U.S.: 3010 Walden Ave., P.O. Box 1325, Buffalo, NY 14269
Canadian: P.O. Box 609, Fort Erie, Ont. L2A 5X3

Mother in a Moment

ALLISON LEIGH

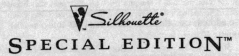

SPECIAL EDITION™

Published by Silhouette Books

America's Publisher of Contemporary Romance

To my local cheerleaders. You know who you are.

And to my editor, Ann Leslie Tuttle, who always manages to make me dig deeper, and never, ever loses her patience.

SILHOUETTE BOOKS

ISBN 0-373-24367-7

MOTHER IN A MOMENT

Copyright © 2000 by Allison Lee Kinnard

This edition published by arrangement with Harlequin Books S.A.

® and TM are trademarks of Harlequin Books S.A., used under license. Trademarks indicated with ® are registered in the United States Patent and Trademark Office, the Canadian Trade Marks Office and in other countries.

Visit Silhouette at www.eHarlequin.com

Printed in U.S.A.

Books by Allison Leigh

Silhouette Special Edition

Stay... #1170
The Rancher and the Redhead #1212
A Wedding for Maggie #1241
A Child for Christmas #1290
Millionaire's Instant Baby #1312
Married to a Stranger #1336
Mother in a Moment #1367

*Men of the Double-C Ranch

ALLISON LEIGH

started early by writing a Halloween play that her grade-school class performed for her school. Since then, though her tastes have changed, her love for reading has not. And her writing appetite simply grows more voracious by the day.

Born in Southern California, she has lived in eight different cities in four different states. She has been, at one time or another, a cosmetologist, a computer programmer and an administrative assistant.

Allison and her husband currently make their home in Arizona, where their time is thoroughly filled with two very active daughters, full-time jobs, pets, church, family and friends. In order to give herself the precious writing time she craves, she burns a lot of midnight oil.

A great believer in the power of love—her parents still hold hands—she cannot imagine anything more exciting to write about than the miracle of two hearts coming together.

IT'S OUR 20th ANNIVERSARY!

December 2000 marks the end of our anniversary year. We hope you've enjoyed the many special titles already offered, and we invite you to sample those wonderful titles on sale this month! 2001 promises to be every bit as exciting, so keep coming back to Silhouette Books, where love comes alive....

Desire

 MAN OF THE MONTH
#1333 Irresistible You
Barbara Boswell

 Freedom Valley
#1334 Slow Fever
Cait London

#1335 A Season for Love
BJ James

#1336 Groom of Fortune
Peggy Moreland

 The Grooms
#1337 Monahan's Gamble
Elizabeth Bevarly

 MILLION DOLLAR MEN
#1338 Expecting the Boss's Baby
Leanne Banks

Romance

 Bachelor Gulch
#1486 Sky's Pride and Joy
Sandra Steffen

#1487 Hunter's Vow
Susan Meier

 THE BRUBAKER BRIDES
#1488 Montana's Feisty Cowgirl
Carolyn Zane

SINGLE DOCTOR DADS
#1489 Rachel and the M.D.
Donna Clayton

STORK EXPRESS
#1490 Mixing Business...with Baby
Diana Whitney

#1491 His Special Delivery
Belinda Barnes

Special Edition

 AND BABY MAKES THREE: THE NEXT GENERATION
#1363 The Delacourt Scandal
Sherryl Woods

#1364 The McCaffertys: Thorne
Lisa Jackson

 #1365 The Cowboy's Gift-Wrapped Bride
Victoria Pade

Rumor Has It... **#1366 Lara's Lover**
Penny Richards

#1367 Mother in a Moment
Allison Leigh

 Here Come the Brides **#1368 Expectant Bride-To-Be**
Nikki Benjamin

Intimate Moments

#1045 Special Report
Merline Lovelace/Maggie Price/Debra Cowan

A Year of Loving Dangerously **#1046 Strangers When We Married**
Carla Cassidy

36 HOURS **#1047 A Very...Pregnant New Year's**
Doreen Roberts

#1048 Mad Dog and Annie
Virginia Kantra

#1049 Mirror, Mirror
Linda Randall Wisdom

#1050 Everything But a Husband
Karen Templeton

Chapter One

"You want me to...*what?*"

Darby White chewed on the inside of her lip, involuntarily taking a step back from the appalled reaction of the tall man standing in front of her. She couldn't blame him, under the circumstances.

Circumstances. She swallowed the knot that had been in her throat for the past few hours and looked away while the social worker again explained to Garrett Cullum what they were doing on his doorstep on what should have been a lovely Minnesota summer evening.

"Accident...fatal...children...Social Services."

Darby looked down the quiet street as the social worker spoke. Most of the houses had two stories and were on modestly sized grassy lots. A few of the yards had picket fences, a few were brightened with flowerbeds.

But no matter how hard she tried focusing on this normal, average neighborhood, attempting to block out the news they'd come to deliver, there was no blocking out the memory of the car accident. She'd heard it and had run out onto the street and seen the mangled vehicles.

Her eyes burned and she turned back to the man in the doorway, who looked shell-shocked. And his gaze, as if he sensed her eyes on him, turned toward her even though Laura Malone was still explaining the course of events that had brought them to his door.

Dark-green, they were. Surrounded by smoky, smudgy lashes, which on a face less masculine would have seemed feminine. And Darby felt a twinge of guilt for noticing such a thing at a time like this—he'd just learned that his sister and brother-in-law had been killed in an automobile accident earlier that day, and she was cataloging his features.

"You were there?" His voice, husky and low-pitched, rolled from where he stood in his open doorway, down the three steps to where Darby stood with the social worker. "At the accident?"

She nodded, but it was her companion who spoke. "Ms. White was first on the scene, Mr. Cullum. Are you sure you wouldn't like to discuss this inside?"

He shook his head, just as he'd done when they'd arrived. He still watched Darby, and her throat went even tighter. "And Elise…my sister spoke to you. Said she wanted *me* to take care of her kids. She said that. Before she—"

Again, Darby nodded. She felt chilled, even though the night was warm. She cleared her throat. "Her only thoughts were of her children."

"Who were safely inside the child-care center where you work."

"Yes. Marc and Elise were—" She hesitated, scrambling for composure. "Were on their way to pick them up. And the accident happened, um, on the corner…outside our building. I'm so sorry," she whispered. "The children—"

"An associate from my office is with the children right now," Laura cut in. "We thought it best until we'd had a chance to speak with you." She had at least twenty years on Darby's twenty-six, but even she looked a little red-eyed. "If you're unable to take your nieces and nephews, they'll be placed in a temporary foster home until we're able to reach their grandfather. We understand he left on a business trip earlier today. His plane is probably just now arriving in Florida, and we've got someone waiting at the airport there to tell him what has happened. We have very good foster homes in Fisher Falls, but it is something that we would all like to avoid, if possible. Family members are almost always preferred."

His square jaw tightened. "How did you know I was here? I've only been in Fisher Falls for two weeks."

"Your business card was in Elise's purse," Darby said. "Your address here was written on the back of it."

"I'm surprised she kept it," he murmured. Then blinked and raked one long-fingered hand through his thick black hair, leaving it standing in rumpled spikes. His shoulders rose and fell heavily as he looked back, into the modest-size house. "I'm not exactly set up for kids here. This place is just a rental."

Darby wasn't sure if he was speaking to them or to

himself. He turned around again and focused those mossy-green eyes on her. "The kids you want me to take in. How old are they?"

Darby blinked, and abruptly gathered herself. Just because he was their uncle didn't mean he had to know their exact ages, she reasoned. He was new to town, as he'd admitted. Perhaps he hadn't seen them in a while.

"Regan is four, Reid is three. The triplets are nine months." She thought she heard him mutter an oath, but decided she'd imagined it. "They're wonderful children, really." Oh, why was she telling this man that? She cared for the Northrop children periodically at the Smiling Faces Child-Care Center; he was their blood. The children had been entrusted to him by their mother's last words; surely he knew how sweet his own nieces and nephews were.

"Mr. Cullum, I know this is a difficult situation. I'm sure we can arrange for any items you may need," Laura inserted calmly. "That is, if you do agree to your sister's wishes. We're not trying to force you to do so. I'm certain your father, once he returns from Florida will be anxious to—"

Darby barely heard the rest of the other woman's words as she watched Garrett Cullum's green eyes harden. No longer soft and mossy-green, they held all the warmth of ice chips. And Darby was glad that he wasn't looking at her just then.

"Where do I pick them up?" he asked abruptly.

The cell phone attached to Laura Malone's hip suddenly chirped to life, and she excused herself. "I'm sorry," she said. "I have to take this. I'm the senior social—"

Garrett waved away Laura's apology and looked at

Darby, clearly expecting her to answer him. "They're still at the center," she told him. "We've got car seats and other things that you can use until…well, until." Darby felt sure that Molly Myers, the center's administrator, wouldn't protest her lending out their precious equipment. And in a few days, when Molly returned from her conference down in Minneapolis, she'd confirm it. Darby figured this infraction of the center's rules was understandable. Considering the circumstances.

Her throat tightened up again and her head ached deep behind her eyes. She drew in a short breath and focused hard on the pickup truck parked in the driveway. "Is that yours?" There was no way he'd be able to cart five children around in it. "We'll use my car," she suggested.

"Why?"

She jumped a little. He'd stepped down the porch and stood next to her. Towering over her. "Car seats." Four of them. Regan was old enough to use a seat belt. It would be a close fit, particularly since Garrett Cullum was broad in the shoulder and long in the leg. He was easily as tall as her brother, and Dane cleared six feet by a good two inches.

There was nothing brotherly about Garrett Cullum, though.

"Mr. Cullum." Laura Malone had finished her call and was holding out a business card. "Darby can take you back to the center. I'm sure she'll help as much as possible in seeing the children settled with you. She's been very helpful today, even fending off some reporters. If we weren't shorthanded already, I'd accompany you myself. I'll contact you when we've got a date to meet with the judge who will finalize the matter of the children.''

Garrett slowly took the card.

"It probably won't be for a week or so," Laura warned. "We're just backed up all over the place with people going away for summer vacations. You'll be assigned a permanent caseworker, too. But if you need anything in the meantime, my number is on the card, plus on the back you'll note the name and numbers of the psychologists working with our department on cases such as this. You'll probably want to talk to—"

He pocketed the card, but his expression was closed. "Thanks."

The social worker nodded, then paused before walking toward her car parked at the curb. Her stoic expression softened for a moment. "Mr. Cullum, Garrett, I know you don't remember me, but I knew your mother. We went to high school together. And I knew Elise and Marc. Not well, but…well, I *am* very sorry for your loss."

Then Darby and Garrett Cullum were alone.

She looked down at her hands, twisted together, as the evening silence seemed to thicken. No amount of training, of schooling, of experience had equipped her for a moment like this. "Perhaps we should go," she finally suggested. Then frowned at the desperation she heard in her own voice. That wouldn't do. Not at all.

Her keys jangled when she pulled them from the pocket of her pleated shorts and she started toward her car. The green paint was beginning to peel and the engine occasionally backfired, but the tires were sound and it held more passengers than the cab of his pickup truck.

"Darby."

She stopped and looked back at him. He hadn't moved one step.

"It *is* Darby. Right?"

She was glad for the darkening twilight. And for the distance between them. "Yes. Darby White." After three months now, she'd gotten to the point where she no longer stumbled over the name each time she used it. Yet the way he was watching her made her feel as if there was a giant warning light flashing on her forehead.

"The driver of the other car." He crossed the small patch of grass that was his front yard. "Phil something, I think Ms. Malone said. He didn't make it, either."

Her fingers closed around the jagged edges of her keys. "No. He didn't."

"His family has probably been notified, too."

Darby swallowed and turned to her car. "I have no idea," she murmured. The lie sat heavily, for she knew that Phil Candela had no family. He'd been too devoted to his job. "I think I heard someone say he was from out of town."

Garrett watched Darby round the aging sedan, purpose in her leggy stride. It was a lot easier to focus on her than think about the news she and the social worker had delivered.

Elise and her husband were dead.

And for reasons only Elise could have explained, she had managed to tell Darby that she wanted *him* to take care of her kids, before she'd slipped from life.

Him. Garrett Cullum. Caldwell Carson's bastard son who'd been shipped out of Fisher Falls nearly twenty years earlier when he'd been only fifteen years old. The half brother Elise had always gone out of her way to avoid, unless she had some specific purpose in tormenting him.

He pulled open the car door and folded himself into the front seat beside Darby. He watched Darby fumble with her keys for a moment, then the engine rumbled reluctantly to life. Maybe her car had more room than his truck, but he had a serious doubt as to whether the engine would survive the trip into the center of town, where he remembered the child-care center was located.

She shifted into gear and set off with only a small jerk, and stared fiercely through the windshield as she drove through the neighborhood. He'd chosen it because it was on the outskirts of town and was one of the few developments around that Caldwell's company, Castle Construction, hadn't built.

Most importantly, though, nobody on this side of town was likely to remember him. He'd come to Fisher Falls with a definite purpose, but the idea of constantly running into people he'd once known hadn't been particularly appealing.

Just as it hadn't been particularly delightful running into Elise the first week he'd arrived. He'd gone into the deli near the temporary office he'd set up, and there she'd been. Sitting alone at a table looking just as pampered and spoiled as she'd been when he was fifteen and she only a year younger.

If she hadn't popped out of her seat and stood in his way, he would have been happy to have pretended not to know her. But she had, and she'd acted as if she was delighted to see him. When he had cynically asked what she wanted, she'd laughed gaily and waved her hand, as if to dismiss his question. But when she'd asked why *he* was in town, he'd told her. Her smile hadn't wavered at all at his clear statement that he was establishing a new branch of his construction company in Fisher Falls, even though she had to know that he would be in direct competition with their father.

And for reasons that still confounded him, he'd ended up giving her his address and phone number here in town when she'd handed over to him a linen business card imprinted with her name and number in gold script.

As if they were likely to call each other up for a chat or something, for Christ's sake.

He pinched the bridge of his nose, remembering that his half sister wouldn't be calling anyone ever again.

"Are you all right?"

He dropped his hand and looked at Darby. "No, I'm not all right." He saw her bite her lip as she focused again on the road ahead.

But he wasn't feeling impatient with her—only with himself. He stifled an oath and tore at his collar again, finally yanking his tie free and pulling it off. He balled it in his fist and looked at her.

The light was gradually fading, but it had been light enough to see her when he'd opened the door to find her and the social worker standing outside. Unlike Laura Malone, who'd been wearing a navy-blue suit, Darby White wore tan shorts and shirt. The shorts were neither too long nor too short, and the legs they revealed were shapely and firm and way too long for someone whose head barely reached his shoulder. Her blue eyes had been moist, and she had a short mop of reddish hair that stuck out at all sorts of angles around her head.

Neither carrot-red nor auburn nor blond, but somewhere in between, the choppy, wavy feathers had captured the setting sun, causing each strand to gleam with fiery light, and she'd looked oddly appealing. Now, in the car's interior, her hair looked like licks of flame against her pale face, and he added *vulnerable* to the mix.

"The kids. What have they been told?" He watched her slender hands tighten even more around the steering wheel, and felt his stomach tighten, too.

"Um, nothing," she said huskily. "We kept them from seeing the cars through the front windows at the center. Laura thought the news might be better coming from you or Mr. Carson."

He exhaled roughly. Great.

She pulled into a well-lit parking lot beside the cheery-looking building, and Garrett couldn't help himself—he looked toward the corner. There was nothing remaining to indicate that a tragedy had occurred there earlier that day. The traffic signal still turned yellow, then red, even though there were no cars there to stop.

He closed his eyes for a moment, thinking of all that hadn't been. And all that wouldn't be.

When he opened them, Darby with her rusty hair and brimming eyes filled his vision. She touched his hand. "It'll be all right."

He doubted it. But still he found his hand turning over, closing around hers. For a lingering moment it helped.

Then she drew away. She ducked her head, but he still saw her swipe her fingers over her cheeks. They went inside through a door that jingled merrily, where the lights were bright and cheerful. Where five little kids waited.

Slept, actually.

The girl with blond curls streaming over her shoulders lay facedown on a blue mat and was obviously the oldest. That would be Regan. And sleeping on a mat beside her, equally blond, but with hair cut short must be Reid.

Garrett shoved his hands in his pockets and stood at a distance as he watched Darby greet the matronly woman who'd been sitting in a rocking chair with a magazine on her lap. The other woman was from Social Services, he assumed, when she shut her magazine with a snap and gathered up a bulging briefcase.

He was glad when Darby quickly and quietly went about gathering up two car seats and pushed them into his arms. Action had always been his preference to inaction.

But when they'd fastened three seats into the back seat and one into the center of the front bench seat, Darby stood back from the car and frowned. "I'm sorry. I should have had you follow in your truck. We're going to be more crowded than I'd thought."

"I'll drive," he said and smoothly plucked the keys she was worrying between her fingers away from her. "You and Regan can fit in one seat belt."

"But—"

"It'll have to do," he said shortly. "The streets of Fisher Falls are all rolled up now. Traffic is nil."

Still, she shook her head. "I think we should split up. Some in my car, some in her—" She turned her head just in time to see the Social Services woman drive away, taking with her any chance of creative carpooling. "Well, fudge."

Garrett felt pretty much the same, though he wouldn't have couched it in such genteel terms. Obviously the Social Services people hadn't felt any qualms about leaving five kids with him. As if the fact that he was their mother's half brother was enough evidence of suitability.

It angered him, suddenly. For all any of them knew, he could be a monster. A hideous parental figure. And this Darby was a child-care worker. Not even an official representative of Social Services. "This is crazy," he muttered, staring at the keys in his hand.

"I know it's little comfort at a time like this, but you will adjust to your loss," Darby said. Her voice was still husky, and Garrett realized that it wasn't just tears that put that velvety-soft rasp in it. "You and Elise must have been very close."

"Close?" He snorted softly. "No, I wouldn't say that." He couldn't begin to figure why he'd even responded to that statement. He'd never been one to speak freely. Not with the few people he considered his friends, and sure as hell not with strangers, even when they came equipped with sympathetic blue eyes and mile-long legs.

Dammit. His sister was dead, he'd actually agreed to take responsibility for five kids who didn't know him from Adam and he was leering at Darby White.

She wasn't even his type. He preferred tall blondes with some curve around their bones. This pint-size woman looked as if she'd poke him with the sharp angles of her shoulders if he got too close.

He realized he was still watching her. Saw the way her eyes widened a bit, the way her lips parted for breath, as if she'd caught his thoughts. She looked shocked.

And why wouldn't she be?

He turned his back on her and went inside the building, where he picked up a padded bag patterned with little blue and yellow ducks. It was stuffed with disposable diapers and brightly colored plastic toys and God knew what else. He carried it to the car and stuck it on the floor in the back seat.

Darby was still standing in the same spot on the other side of the car from him. Now she just looked puzzled. "Then why?"

"Why what?" But he knew.

She moistened her lips and shook her head, looking away. "It's really none of my business."

Since he agreed with her there, he left it at that.

Only she didn't.

She followed him into the center and stood beside him, looking down at the children sleeping on their mats. Across the spacious room, three well-padded little bottoms stuck up in the air from three cribs where they, too, slept.

"If you weren't close," Darby asked in a soft voice, "why would your sister want you to raise her children?"

Chapter Two

Why, indeed?

Garrett had no idea. Elise couldn't possibly have known what she'd been saying. Or, in the chaos of the moment, Darby had somehow misunderstood. All he knew was that he was going to take full advantage of the situation.

"Well," she finally said, when it became clear that he wasn't going to answer, "I'm sure that it will all work out. When your dad returns, you can—"

"I don't have a dad."

"Oh. But, I thought—Laura indicated that you—"

"Caldwell Carson was Elise's dad. To me he was just the married guy who knocked up my mother. Everybody in this town knew he was responsible, but he's the only one to pretend it never happened. And the only thing I need to work out is loading these guys into the car and getting them back to my place. So are you going to help or not?''

Her soft lips closed. Without looking at him, she knelt down beside Reid and gently gathered up the boy into her arms and carried him out into the night.

Garrett blew out a breath and crouched next to Regan. She jerked and blinked and stared at him through eyes that were as brown as her mother's had been.

He felt a swift and unexpected knot form inside him. Grief. Where the hell did it come from? He didn't like it. So he shoved it back into oblivion and warily eyed the little girl. As warily as she regarded him, he noticed.

''Who're you?'' Suspicion vibrated from her small person.

''I'm your uncle Garrett.''

Her face became fearful, and she pushed away from him, yelling, ''Stranger!'' over and over again. She ran to Darby, who'd reentered the building, and practically jumped into her arms. She twined her legs around Darby's waist and buried her blond head against Darby's shoulder.

''Maybe you could get the triplets,'' she suggested calmly. ''I'll wait in the car with Regan and Reid.''

Sure. Get the triplets. No sweat.

Right.

There was nothing for him to do but agree, so he turned toward the cribs lining the wall. Cheerful balloons and kites had been painted above the cribs, and he focused on them as he walked closer.

If he was a drinker, he'd be thinking about now that this was all some alcohol-induced hallucination. Some nightmarish fog that he would wake up from, sooner or later. But when he stood next to the cribs and looked down at two scrunched up butts and one wide-eyed baby, who was now chewing on the corner of a blanket, Garrett knew there was no waking from this nightmare.

He was thirty-five years old, for God's sake. Why did looking into the round little face of a nine-month-old tot with a head nearly as bald as the cue ball on his pool table back home in Albuquerque make him want to head the opposite direction? Fast.

The baby's mouth parted in a grin, baring several stubby little teeth. He…*she?*…stood up and wrapped little starfish hands around the edge of the crib and bounced its little knees. Garrett's unease wasn't going anywhere, he knew, so he just reached out and picked up the kid, holding it at arm's length as he strode outside to the car. The kid didn't seem to mind. It grinned, drooled and wriggled its legs as if Garrett was some longtime friend.

Darby was standing by the car, and he pushed the baby at her. She had little choice but to accept, and Garrett went back inside, leaving her to fasten the child into one of the safety seats crammed into the back seat.

The other two babies were still sound asleep. Garrett scooped them both up, hoped they wouldn't wake and start screaming at him, too, and took them outside.

By the time he pulled into his driveway next to his pickup, all of them having been packed into Darby's car so snugly that he felt some real sympathy for sardines, his head was pounding with the force of jackhammers.

And the fun was just beginning.

"Mr. Cullum?" Darby was looking at him over Regan's sleeping form. "I think we should get the children inside."

He shoved open the car door and unfolded himself. "I'm gonna need a van," he muttered, and nearly cringed at the notion.

Getting the children inside the house proved to be nearly as much work as getting them settled inside the car. But finally the job was done. The triplets were situated in the center of his wide bed—the only piece of furniture he'd acquired new when he'd moved into the rental. It was king-size, extra-long and fit him to a *T*. Right now his long, fat pillows were lined around the edges like some puffy corral, to keep the sleeping triplets in the center, and the likelihood of him getting a decent night's sleep grew even dimmer.

Tad, Keely and Bridget. One boy and two girls.

"They look like three peas in a pod," he muttered, staring at the sight from the doorway. Darby had put Regan and Reid in the second bedroom. Fortunately, it had come furnished with twin beds.

"You'll get used to them," Darby assured. "And you don't have to dress them alike that way just because their—" Her voice broke off awkwardly.

"Because their mother did," Garrett finished flatly. Trust Elise—pretty, proper, pampered—to dress her triplets alike. "You don't have to avoid her name."

"I wasn't." But her distressed expression told a different story. "You'll be able to tell the triplets apart before long," she reassured.

"Sure," Garrett agreed abruptly. "When it's time to change a diaper, I'll know whether I've got Tad in hand or not."

Her lips twitched the moment before she turned

away. "If it helps, Keely is the only one with eight teeth already."

"Great. Another clue." Garrett followed Darby down the narrow stairs, back into the living room, where they'd already dumped the diaper bag and the assortment of other items she'd filched from the child-care center.

She glanced around. "I must go. Did you put my car keys somewhere?"

He slowly drew them out of his pocket and held them up in the air. "You're responsible for this situation, Darby White. You don't think I'm gonna let you go all that easily, do you?"

Responsible.

Darby felt the blood drain from her head, and her knees wobbled. She stared at Garrett. How could he know? How could anyone know?

He was swearing under his breath and pushing her into a chair, nudging her head down between her knees. She pushed at his hands, but he held her firm. She squirmed. "What are you doing?"

"You looked like you were gonna pass out."

He bent his knees and crouched in front of her, finally allowing Darby to lift her head. But he was so close she could see the flecks of brown in his green eyes, and she wanted to lower her head once more. Her throat tightened again. "Mr. Cullum, I don't know how you—"

"Garrett."

"I...what?"

"Call me Garrett. Seems stupid to be so formal under the circumstances."

Not even Dane had lashes as long as this man's, and Dane was so handsome Darby used to tease him about being pretty. She swallowed nervously. "I'm terribly sorry about—"

"Dumping five kids on me? Don't feel sorry for me," he murmured. "Feel sorry for *them*. And if it weren't for you speaking up about what Elise told you, they wouldn't be saddled with an uncle who doesn't have a clue what to do with 'em." He straightened. "You can't just abandon us now."

The room swam again and Darby pressed her fingertips to her closed eyes. From blind panic to pitiful relief in the span of a heartbeat was almost more than she could take.

She moistened her lips and dropped her hands, looking up at him. He'd removed his jacket some time ago, and the sleeves of his white linen shirt were folded up his forearms. He looked grim, tired and appealing. And she was appalled at herself for even noticing that at a time like this. For all she knew, he had a wife tucked away somewhere. Or a fiancée. Or a harem.

He also looked something else, she realized with a start. Beneath his steady, green gaze he was just as panicked as she'd felt. And why not? His life had changed today.

She sat up. "Mr. Cull—Garrett, you do have a choice regarding the children. Laura did say that your brother-in-law had no family on his side, but obviously you're not the only remaining relative of the children. Your...Mr. Carson is probably on his way back from his business trip, if he hasn't arrived already. I'm sure between the two of you, you'll manage to—"

"Have you met him?"

"Well, no, actually. I know of him, of course. You can't live in Fisher Falls and not know who Caldwell Carson is. He *is* the mayor, after all. And if not for that, I've heard his company built more than half the homes in the state.''

"Yeah, he's a busy boy, Caldwell is.'' He ran his hand around the back of his neck. ''And between the two of us, we'll be working out exactly nothing. The kids are with me. They'll stay with me.'' His lips thinned. ''It's what Elise wanted, right?''

Darby nodded. It was the one thing she could confirm with complete honesty. And now that job done, it was time for her to go. To remove herself from the situation before she brought more harm to innocent people.

Harm. Such an inadequate word for what she'd caused.

"I need to go.'' She stood and held out her hand for her keys, but he didn't drop them into her palm, and unease rippled through her. ''My keys?''

They jingled, sounding loud in the silence of the house, when he finally released them into her hand. She pushed them into her pocket and headed for the door. ''Good luck with the children.''

"Meaning you think I'll need it.''

"If one of the triplets wakens during the night, I suggest giving a bottle. I saw some cans of formula in the diaper bag as well as clean bottles. It's premixed. Just pour it in the bottle. The children will probably take a while to settle into a new—'' her throat clamped tight ''—a new routine. Just give yourselves plenty of time to, ah, to adjust,'' she finished huskily. She didn't dare look at Garrett. If she did she would start crying.

And if she started crying, she wasn't sure if she could stop.

The past few months had been so calm. So quiet. She'd started to breathe again. And now this. Elise and

Marc had been young, in their prime, with five innocent children completing their home. They hadn't deserved this.

And she felt guilty for even fearing that her brief period of peace might be threatened as a result.

"You know the kids pretty well." Garrett's voice stopped her as she pushed open the screen door. "And they know you."

Darby nodded. It seemed ridiculous to tell him good-night. There was nothing good about this day. "The children usually spend two or three half-days a week at the center. You'll probably want to sign them up full-time. But I should warn you that there is a waiting list. You might have better luck looking at some of the other places in town if that's the route you want to go."

His expression didn't change, but she knew without a single doubt that he was cursing inside his head. Her brother, Dane, got that same look when he was inordinately frustrated.

He'd worn that look a lot around Darby before she'd finally found some backbone and left home three months ago.

Her gaze focused on Garrett, and her shoulders sagged. If she had found her backbone and stayed at home, where everyone had insisted she'd belonged—save her great-aunt Georgie, that is—then today's events would never have occurred. The children sleeping in the bedrooms of this simple, boxy house would be tucked in under the watchful eye of their mother and father—instead of the grimly determined one of their uncle.

"I wouldn't have to worry about waiting lists if you'd come here to watch the kids."

She was more tired than she thought, because he made no sense whatsoever. "I already have a job. I work at Smiling Faces, Mr. Cullum."

"Garrett. You could work here instead. I'll match your salary."

"I...*no*. No, I'm sorry. That's simply not possible." She stepped out onto the porch and quickly shut the screen door.

It was insane. She couldn't even contemplate it. Working at the center was one thing. Being this man's...nanny, was entirely another.

He followed her. Right over to her car. "Why not? Do you have kids of your own?"

Her stomach tightened. "No."

"A husband who'd object? A lover?"

"I'm not married."

His lids lowered. "And...?"

Her cheeks burned. She sidled around him and yanked open the car door. It squealed. "Don't you have a wife or...someone who can watch the children for you?"

"If I had a wife, I wouldn't need a nanny."

"Perhaps she has a demanding career."

"There is no career. No wife. I'm a harmless, single male. I pay my taxes on time, haven't broken any laws lately and shower at least once a month whether I need it or not."

She fumbled her keys from her pocket and sank into the seat, frowning harder.

"Don't you care about the children?"

"Of course I do!" She drew in a sharp breath. "Which is not the point." She tried to pull the door closed, but he folded one hand over the top and held it fast. She looked from his hand to his face. But that made her breathless in a way she didn't dare examine, and she looked back at his hand. "I'd like to leave, Mr. Cullum."

His fingers slowly straightened, though he didn't remove his hand completely. "Double your salary."

She yanked the door closed. The window was still lowered. "Don't be ridiculous. This isn't about money."

"No, it's about five kids who don't deserve to wake up tomorrow with no parents."

His words hit her like a blow to her midsection. Her hand trembled so badly it took her two tries to fit the key in the ignition. The engine sputtered, died.

"Darby, you obviously cared enough about them to see that Elise's wishes were followed. Just consider the idea, would you?"

Even if she did consider it, what good would it do? The children would become attached to her and she to them. When she had to leave—and she *would*—it would be just one more loss in their young lives that they neither deserved nor expected.

She'd done what she could when she'd run out onto the street that afternoon. She'd given CPR. She'd applied tourniquets that had done no good. She'd avoided one reporter, sicced a police officer on another and tried not to completely lose her wits when she'd recognized poor Phil as the driver of the other car. She'd known he must have died instantly.

She'd cradled Elise's head in her arms as the injured woman had urgently whispered about her children. She'd told the police, then Social Services, about Elise's last words.

There wasn't anything more that Darby could do.

Nothing that she could undo.

So the best thing for her to do was go. This man, Elise's brother, would rise to the task of caring for his new charges. She could see it in his face. And just because she was still shaking and distressed over the day's events didn't give her any excuse to sugar-coat her own involvement.

She turned the ignition again, holding her breath until the engine caught. She looked up at Garrett as she put the car into reverse.

And felt herself waver yet again.

The children would be confused and desperately missing their mommy and daddy. Their lives had been torn to pieces through no fault of their own.

Her hands tightened around the steering wheel and she moistened her lips. If she was careful, if she re-membered her…her place, maybe she could—

A movement behind them had her automatically glancing in the rearview mirror. The sight of a white van pulling up at the curb was like a dousing with icy water. The side of the van was painted with the col-orful logo of the local television station.

"I can't help you, Garrett. I'm sorry."

She didn't look at him as she pulled out of the driveway and drove away. In her mirror, she saw someone step from the van and approach Garrett.

Naturally. The mayor's long-absent son had re-turned to town just in time to become the unexpected guardian of his nieces and nephews. In a small place like Fisher Falls, that was big news.

If she didn't stay away from the scene, the news would grow even bigger. And Darby couldn't face that.

Not even for those sweet kids.

Not even for a man like Garrett Cullum.

Chapter Three

"I'm going to go over and see Darby White. She won't refuse in person." Garrett looked across the metal desk to his assistant as he hung up the phone. He'd just been refused child care from the last center in Fisher Falls. And this one had been run by a church. "No room" seemed to be the stock answer in this town. But Garrett knew better. "We can't help out the black-sheep son of our beloved mayor" was what they really meant.

Carmel Delgado rolled her eyes and huffed. "She's already refused you."

Didn't he know it. His temporary office was housed in a trailer on the building site of what would soon be G&G Construction's seventh office, and rather than being filled with desks and filing cabinets for his staff, one end was filled with a playpen, rocking horse and an enormous cardboard box of toys. A box that, he noted absently, the triplets were more interested in chewing on than anything. For now, thankfully, the kids seemed quiet and content enough with their lunch.

"I suppose this means I get to watch 'em for you while you're gone."

"Consider it practice for when you and Enrico finally get hitched and have babies." He yanked open one drawer. Then another, looking for his keys.

Carmel snorted delicately. "Nobody's gonna rope me into marriage. Not even hunky Enrico." She held out one finger. The set of keys hung from her long orange-painted nail. "And back to the point—babysitting isn't in my job description."

He grabbed the keys. "You're my assistant. So assist."

"I want a raise," she called after him as he left the office, and the fearsome five, behind.

Garrett ignored her as he headed for the new Suburban he'd luckily found at one of the car lots in town. It held the fearsome five and it wasn't a van, so he was satisfied.

The truth was, no matter how much Carmel complained, he'd have been sunk without her the past few days. If anyone deserved a raise, it was his flamboyant assistant. But he needed her doing what she was paid to do, not playing nanny to the fearsome five, nor fending off the good town mayor.

Bringing the kids to the office was not a workable solution. They were a distraction to all of his staff, not just Carmel. They had bids to get out, a subcontractor to fire and fifty other things that had slid because he'd been too busy shoveling mashed peas into ravenous little mouths, and changing diapers.

Well, Carmel had changed most of the diapers, he acknowledged as he wheeled the Suburban over the ruts in the dirt road leading to and from the building site. *Definitely* not in her job description.

He had to find an alternative, and Darby White was it. He'd exhausted every other avenue.

Everyone had their price. He would just have to find out what hers was.

Ten minutes later he was walking through the front door of Smiling Faces Child-Care Center. The noise hit him first. A baby crying. A lot of childish, squealing laughter. Someone singing.

Holy God. Give him the chorus of hammer and nails over this racket.

"Can I help you?" A young woman standing behind the long counter separating the entry from the rest of the center widened her eyes and smiled hopefully. She was tall, and had thick blond hair streaming down around her shoulders.

He felt not one speck of interest. He had more important things to take care of. "I'm here to see Darby White."

Her smile dimmed a fraction. She looked over her shoulder, scanning the room. But Garrett had already spotted Darby's distinctive hair, and he rounded the waist-high gate.

"Wait. You can't just go back— Okaaay, I guess you can."

Garrett stepped through the chaos and stopped behind Darby. She was standing in a circle, holding hands with a half dozen kids who looked no older than Reid. They were singing as their circle revolved.

When she was opposite him, her feet stopped. Surprise widened her eyes. Stiffened her shoulders. The children giggled and let go, forming their own wobbly circle without her.

"Garrett. Did you bring the children in today, after all?"

"No. I spoke with your administrator. Molly? Yesterday. The waiting list for full-time care is six months long." In six months, he and the kids would be back in New Mexico where child-care would be more easily solved since Caldwell's damned influence didn't stretch quite that far. Since Garrett had his own share of influence there. "The best I can get is the two hours a day three times a week that Elise had already set up. But you knew that."

She didn't deny it. "How are they?"

"Reid won't sleep at night, and Regan hates me." Yet they'd both screamed bloody murder when he'd tried to get them ready to bring them to Smiling Faces for their regular time. They didn't seem to want to let him out of their sight. Call him a coward, but he'd backed down and instead carted them all to the trailer-office.

Darby pressed her lips together. "Of course Regan doesn't hate you."

"My assistant is about ready to quit unless I arrange something more suitable than bringing the fearsome five to work with me."

Her chin tilted. "There's nothing fearsome about your nieces and nephews. You've told them...I assume."

"Regan is the only one old enough to have some concept of what it means." He hadn't realized Darby's eyes were quite so blue. "That's what the psychologist said. I think that all the kids really understand is that their mom and dad left and didn't come back."

"It's a lot of changes for them."

"Which you could make easier if you'd help me."

Darby looked around. She wasn't surprised in the least that they were the focus of numerous interested stares. Anyone who looked as good as this man did, guaranteed plenty of interest.

It didn't bear thinking about that she was interested enough to take a good, long look at him herself. It had been two years since she'd stood next to a man and felt even the slightest flicker. This was beyond a recipe for disaster, though.

She moistened her lips and angled her back against Beth's avid stare. It didn't take a genius to know what the pretty blond receptionist would be gossiping about next. The woman's mouth was constantly running, and Darby gave her as wide a berth as humanly possible considering they worked at the same place. "Garrett, I can't discuss this with you here. Everyone is watching us."

"Then where? I'm not leaving you alone until I get the answer I need."

"Find someone else!" She lowered her voice and drew him to the rear of the room where the cribs were pushed against the wall. "There are other child-care centers in Fisher Falls. Smiling Faces isn't the only one. There are referral services. Family child-care in private homes. I'm not the only person in town capable of solving your problem. Find another nanny." She lifted her shoulder. "Beth, the blonde over there? She'd take you up in a heartbeat if you asked her."

"She'd be too busy figuring out how to get in my bed to watch the kids."

Darby flushed. It was probably true. And he obviously didn't think he needed to worry about Darby on that score. Big surprise. On her own, she'd never managed to attract much male interest.

"You're the only one in town who didn't think twice about carrying out Elise's wishes," he said.

"So?"

His slashing eyebrows pulled together. "You really don't know, do you?"

She dashed her hair off her forehead. "Know what?"

"Caldwell owns this town and nearly everyone in it."

"He is our mayor. People are naturally loyal to him."

"He wants custody of the children. He filed a suit for them even before they put my sister and her husband in the ground yesterday," Garrett said flatly.

She sighed. Custody battles were never pretty.

"I haven't lived here since I was fifteen," he continued, "and those people who *do* remember me, don't do it with fondness. So let's just say that I'm not exactly overrun with friends I can count on to help me out."

"Well, maybe the best answer is for their grandfather to have them," Darby reasoned. "I'm sure your sister had her reasons for saying what she did, but if Mayor Carson wants them and you're not equipped for caring for them— It's nothing to be ashamed of, Garrett. The important thing here is the children's welfare. Right?"

"She had good reasons." A muscle ticked in his jaw. "Just because he's mayor doesn't mean he is a decent parent. Elise probably knew he'd ruin them just like he ruined us. There's a custody hearing scheduled for next Wednesday to rule on the temporary order put in place when Elise died. At least help me out until then. It's not even a week away.''

A week, she thought. What would one week mean?

A lot, her saner self argued. A person's entire life could change in an instant. Compared to that, a week—six days, actually—could be an eternity.

''You don't even know me,'' she argued. ''How do you know I won't steal the silver or something while you're at work?''

''It's not my silver. House is rented, remember?''

She frowned.

''Molly Myers has already vouched for you. So has Laura Malone and everyone else I've spoken with. You may have only been in town a short while, but you've managed to make an impression.''

She stilled. ''You've been checking on me.''

He didn't deny it. ''You're living with Georgina Vansant. If that's not a character reference, I don't know what is. I've heard that she's having some health problems right now, but I doubt if she's suddenly begun suffering fools.''

''I don't live with Georgie. She lets me stay in her gatehouse.'' Insisted on it, in fact. Georgie thought that Darby needed the independence after all that had happened. Darby had offered to stay with her dear old aunt in Georgie's beautiful main house, but she knew it made Georgie happier to think that she was getting her feet under her.

''Close enough. Six days, Darby. I'll settle for that if it's all I can get. Don't do it for me, even. Do it for the kids.''

She pushed her tongue against her teeth. As a child she'd understood what it felt like to be a pawn in someone else's chess game, and as far as she could tell, it seemed that Garrett and Caldwell were gearing up for a whale of a game. And the children, as always happened, would be the ones to suffer.

But their suffering would never be an issue if the accident hadn't happened in the first place.

She sighed and looked up at him. Trouble, she reminded herself. Nothing but trouble. This man, no matter how fascinating his mossy-green eyes were, was undoubtedly one attractive bundle of trouble. Which is something she needed to avoid.

But she'd told him to put the children's welfare first. Could she do less after what she'd caused?

She could handle a week, couldn't she? She wouldn't be foolish enough to lose her heart again to children that would never be hers. She certainly wouldn't lose her heart to this man she wasn't sure she even liked.

"Would you need someone from say, nine to five?" she asked rather desperately. "Or earlier? Children can wake very early and perhaps you'd need someone—"

"Around the clock," he said smoothly. "That wouldn't be a problem, would it? You said you're not encumbered with a relationship."

She frowned. "That isn't the point, Garrett. I can't…live with you." Not even for six days.

"Why not? My business keeps me busy enough that I'm hardly around anyway."

"You've taken on responsibility for five children," she countered warily. "Surely you plan to be around some?"

"The children will be provided for. I can afford it."

"But will they be loved?" She closed her hand over his arm. "Garrett, if you don't plan to love those kids, why on earth are you rearranging everyone's lives so you can keep them, when your father is obviously willing to do so himself?''

He looked at her hand on his arm, and she followed his gaze. His arm was roped with muscle and tendon and was as warm as the sunshine. She dropped her hand, curling her fingers against the tingle that lingered.

He was silent for a moment. ''Because I stood over my sister's fresh grave yesterday and promised her that I would not fail her.''

Suddenly her heart ached. Simply ached. ''She knew that. Before she—'' She swallowed. ''Elise said you always kept your promises.''

A shadow came and went in his eyes. ''Then help me not fail her kids,'' he said simply.

Her resolve swayed. Maybe she did like him. A little. ''All right,'' she gave in. ''But only until next Wednesday.''

His smile wasn't wide. It wasn't gloating or triumphant or anything else she might have expected in the face of her agreement. What it was, she decided, was a crinkle beside his eyes. A look that said *thanks*.

A look that would disappear should he ever learn that three people had died—including his own sister— because of Darby's presence in Fisher Falls.

Chapter Four

By the time Darby pulled her car to a stop at the curb in front of Garrett's house later that evening, she had convinced herself that she'd made a monumental error in judgment.

She hadn't even been able to talk it over with Georgie. When she'd gone up to the house to see her, Georgie had been sleeping, thanks to the latest round of meds she was receiving for her condition. So she'd had to content herself with leaving a note for Georgie with her homecare nurse.

For now Darby was on her own with this decision.

She looked at Garrett's house and feared she'd decided badly.

Why on earth had she agreed to this? Six days, six hours, six minutes. It was all too much for her to contemplate. To stay in that house there, with the golden light spilling from the front picture window, for even the shortest period of time was only asking for trouble.

Her boss, Molly, hadn't exactly been delighted, either, when Darby had requested the necessary days off from work. Smiling Faces was at its capacity, and extra staff simply wasn't available. But Molly had softened when Darby had admitted that she was trying to help out the Northrop children. She'd even looked at Darby with a speculative look that Darby had had no trouble deciphering.

She'd seen that look often enough in Georgie's eyes, too. Whenever she started thinking of suitable male companions for Darby, her eyes turned sparkly and sly. If Darby *had* been able to talk the situation over with her elderly aunt, Georgie would have probably been delighted.

Frankly, she didn't need Molly or Georgie conjuring notions of Darby and Garrett. It would be ridiculous. Even if the situation weren't what it was, Darby was not in the market for a man. She had enough on her plate just keeping herself focused, thank you very much. She had no desire to offer her heart up on a chopping block again. The last time she'd done so, two years earlier, had been her final graduate course in that foolishness. She'd finally learned her lesson.

She looked at Garrett's house again. She blew out a noisy breath and pushed open her car door, reaching in the back seat for the overnight bag she'd packed. She slung the strap over her shoulder. The bag didn't weigh a lot. She didn't need much, after all. Six days spent taking care of children didn't require much fanciness in the fashion arena.

She had barely started up the sidewalk leading to the house when she heard a baby's infuriated yowl.

She hurried her pace, bounding up the steps to the screen door. She lifted her hand to knock, then jumped back when the door flew open.

Darby looked down to see Regan a moment before the little girl pounced on her legs, nearly taking them both right back down the porch steps. Darby hastily grabbed the rail for balance and realized that another person had appeared in the doorway, too.

She patted Regan's back and tried to mentally force blood to circulate through the girl's strangling grip on her legs. "Hello. I'm—"

"Hallelujah, extra hands have arrived. You must be Darby. I'm Carmel."

Before Darby could blink, the other woman—shorter than Darby, and that was saying something—wrapped her hand around Darby's arm and dragged her and Regan through the door. "Garrett," she called over her shoulder as she pulled the door shut and fastened the latch. "The savior has arrived." Liquid brown-black eyes turned back to Darby. "Thank God you're here. We're drowning."

Darby flushed. Regan finally let go of Darby's leg and lifted her arms. She picked up the child and tried not to wonder too hard over *who* Carmel was.

"We don't got a pool anymore to get drownded in," Regan whispered worriedly in Darby's ear. "Are we gonna go 'way like Mommy and Daddy?"

Darby hugged the girl and set her on her feet, keeping hold of her little hand. It didn't matter who Carmel was. Darby's purpose here was clear in her mind. "No," she told Regan calmly. "Where's your uncle Garrett?"

"In the kitchen," Carmel answered. She straightened her shiny red shirt and patted down her equally flaming shoulder-length curls before turning on her spiked heel and clattering down the tiled hallway toward, Darby presumed, the kitchen.

Feeling like a faded dishrag in the wake of Carmel's, well, *color,* Darby followed. She noticed the playpen in the living room, the toys littering the floor, the full laundry basket sitting on the couch. The kitchen was no better. The bottom cupboard doors were all opened, and pots and pans and plastic bowls and lids spilled out onto the linoleum.

It looked as if an earthquake had hit.

And smack in the middle of it sat the triplets, lined up in their trio of high chairs. Keely was the one caterwauling, but Garrett, who sat in front of the high chairs on a straight-back kitchen chair with green goop dripping down the front of his white shirt appeared to be the one in true pain.

He looked over at Darby, and his face was so grim and determined that she had to fight a smile. Then he raked his hand through his hair, leaving a streak of green lumps behind, and Regan made a little gasping sound. As if she wanted to laugh but couldn't quite get the sound out.

"Nice look for you there, boss," Carmel said smoothly. She was gathering up an enormous neon-yellow purse, clearly planning her escape route. "Too bad the folks from *GQ* aren't here with their cameras."

"Darby, this pain in the rear is my assistant, Carmel Delgado. Carmel, Darby White."

"Nice to meet you," Carmel said cheerfully. "I'm outta here to my nice motel room that has a *working* air conditioner and room service for dinner. Unlike this place."

"Carmel—"

"See you tomorrow!" She clattered back out of the room. In seconds they heard the slam of the screen door followed by the roar of a car engine.

Darby realized she was staring at Garrett and quickly looked down at Regan. It was well after eight o'clock. And the house was definitely warm, still retaining the heat of the day even though it was very pleasant outside now. "Have any of you eaten dinner?"

Regan shook her head.

"Where's Reid?"

"Digging up the backyard, most likely. It seems to be something that he really excels at," Garrett answered. He'd turned back to the babies. Keely's yelling had, thankfully, subsided.

"Go get Reid," Darby instructed Regan. "And wash your hands, then come and sit at the table."

The little girl didn't look thrilled, but she went. Darby set her overnighter on the floor by the wall and looked at Garrett.

"Don't say it," he said flatly. "They should have been in bed an hour ago. And I have been trying to give them dinner for two hours now. I was gonna order pizza or something, but Regan vetoed everything I suggested. Whatever she says, Reid pipes right along with her."

"Actually, I was going to say that you might have better luck with the triplets if you gave them some finger food. They're at the age where they want to feed themselves. Or try, anyway."

"Which would explain why they've been throwing their food back at me," he muttered. He scooted back the chair and rose, seeming to realize what a mess his shirt was. Dusky color rose in his throat, and Darby told herself she was *not* charmed. This was just a job.

She walked purposefully to the refrigerator and opened the door. The offerings were slim, but he did have eggs and milk. She pulled out both and set them on the counter, then began opening cupboards—the ones up top that hadn't already been divested of their contents. "Why don't you get cleaned up, too," she suggested without looking his way.

He went.

And Darby breathed easier. She found a clean dish-cloth and wiped up the mess the triplets had already made, then gave them each a handful of dry cereal. Regan trooped in with a disheveled Reid, and they disappeared in a room off the kitchen. She heard water running, then giggles.

Darby figured she'd go into the bathroom later and find bubbles and water flooding half the room, but she didn't care. The children were giggling and the happy sound warmed her. Then, overhead, she heard a hideous, groaning rattle of pipes.

A shower, she realized. And a prompt vision of Garrett pulling off his food-decorated shirt popped into her mind.

She shook her head sharply and reached for the waffle iron that sat on the floor under the table. Waffles and scrambled eggs for dinner wasn't exactly imaginative. But it would have to do for now. Until she could get to the grocery store and stock up on—

"Whoa, Nellie," she muttered out loud. All she needed to worry about was the next few days. After that, Mr. Garrett Cullum and his crew would have to depend on other arrangements. Darby was only here as a stopgap.

* * *

Garrett paused in the doorway to the kitchen. It looked almost like the kitchen that had come with the house when he'd first rented it a few weeks ago. Except for the row of high chairs and the kids, that was.

And except for a rusty-haired sprite who'd worked wonders in a bare half hour. Then, as if he'd cleared his throat or stomped his foot to announce his presence, Darby turned around and looked at him.

His chest locked up for a second. She'd rolled up the short sleeves of her tan T-shirt, displaying the sleek, perfect curve of her shoulders. He managed to smile crookedly and drag his eyes from the T-shirt that clung damply to her chest. So she wasn't quite as bony as he'd thought. "Looks like you were target practice for someone yourself," he said.

Darby's eyes flicked to Regan, and she smiled gently. "Just a little accident with our water glasses," she said as she moved toward the table.

Garrett realized she was setting a loaded plate onto the table, and he looked away from Regan's ducked head. Regan had probably had the same "accident" as she'd had when she'd dumped her milk on Garrett the day before.

"It's not much," Darby murmured, gesturing a little so he knew the plate was for him.

Salivating over the nanny was *not* an option. So he focused on the food, instead. "Are you kidding? I didn't have to fix it, and I didn't have to order it at a restaurant. Looks great." He sat down at the table and reached for the syrup. It was in a tidy little pitcher, not the entire bottle stuck in the center of the table the way his mother's cousin would have done it. He dumped the warm syrup on his waffle and watched

Darby wipe sticky hands and faces. "But you don't need to cook for me."

Her eyebrows rose as she glanced at him. Then she turned her pretty eyes away again. "I have to feed them and myself. You're just one more," she said evenly.

Which put him nicely in his place. *Just one more.* Nobody special. No surprise there.

Over his fork he watched Darby pluck Keely from the high chair and settle her on the floor. He thought it was Keely, anyway. She didn't do anything but crawl speedily out of the kitchen.

"I think I should get a big old black marker and write their names on their shirts," he said. "Easier than counting teeth or checking under the diaper."

Darby smiled faintly as she wiped up another sticky little face.

Regan and Reid were watching him from their seats across the table. Finding him wanting, no doubt. He smiled at them and received the glorious response of Regan, immediately followed by Reid, scrambling out of their chairs and racing from the room. He gave up the smile and found Darby looking at him.

"They need time."

"They need their parents," he countered grimly. "Unfortunately, that isn't gonna happen."

Darby's eyes looked wet. She blinked and turned away, then with the other two babies propped on both hips she followed the children who'd already escaped.

He thought about following, too. But the restored-to-order kitchen seemed to mock him. In just a short time Darby had cooked, fed and cleaned up. Even the living room had been restored to some semblance of order. She was utterly competent, just as he'd known she would be. And the kids hadn't looked at her with anything but trust despite the spilled water across her shirt.

He might be the uncle, but just as Regan had said, he *was* the stranger here.

Appetite gone, he finished eating, anyway, then rinsed his dishes and added them to the dishwasher that Darby had left all ready to go. He flipped the switch, and it groaned to life.

Upstairs, thanks to walls he considered miserably thin, he could hear the children talking and the lower murmur of Darby's husky voice. He stood at the base of the staircase and listened for a moment. He wrapped his hand around the plain wood banister. Put his foot on the first step.

But he went no farther.

Then the telephone rang and he went to answer it, using the phone in the downstairs den that also served as an office. It was one of his subcontractors calling from Dallas, wanting to go over some details of a shopping center project there. By the time he finished with the call, it was nearly ten and he'd managed to put away whatever it was that had stopped him from going up the stairs earlier.

The sight of Darby sitting on the lumpy couch in the living room reminded him, though. What had she said at Smiling Faces?

I can't live with you.

He'd glossed over it at the time. But now, it was all he could think about. Six days or not, she was staying under his roof.

She saw him, and if anything, seemed to draw even more tightly into the corner of the couch. She'd replaced her tan T-shirt with a white one. Big and baggy and eclipsing.

"I'm not the bad guy, you know," he said. He sat down on the fake-leather recliner with a rip in the arm.

Surprise widened her eyes. "Did I say you were?"

"It's not exactly cold here in the house, and you're huddling there like you expect to be devoured by the wolf."

She immediately straightened out her legs from beneath her. "Wolves have never been interested in me," she demurred.

Sleek thighs, curving calves, narrow ankles hidden beneath little, white folded-down socks. He was better off with her legs hidden beneath the folds of that gigantic T-shirt.

He looked at the empty fireplace, thinking she'd met some mighty stupid wolves. "The kids asleep?"

"Yes. Where did you get the cribs for the triplets?"

"From Elise's house. Laura managed to arrange it. Yesterday after the funeral."

She fell silent. Her fingers pleated the hem of her shirt. "The, uh, the master bedroom is pretty full, up there. What with the cribs. And the...bed."

"Wall to wall," he agreed absently. She really did have pretty knees. And in the light from the lamp behind the couch her skin looked like cream.

"And the other room with the twin beds. Regan and Reid seem very comfortable there."

"Except Reid doesn't seem to sleep through the night any better than the triplets do."

She chewed her lip and looked away. "Well."

Then it dawned on him, and amusement unexpectedly hit him. "You can use the master," he said. "I'll use the pullout in the den."

"Oh. I don't want to put you out of your bed."

"You just don't want to sleep in the same room as Bridget, Tad and Keely."

Her cheeks colored. "No, of course I don't mind that. I mean, I'm here to take care of them, after all."

"But?"

"Perhaps we could put the triplets in the, uh, the den. And I'll sleep there with them."

"The den is smaller than the second bedroom upstairs. The simplest solution is for you to take my bed." He watched her closely. "Unless sleeping in my bed is a problem?" He knew exactly how that sounded. And damned if he didn't care. No, that wasn't right. He *did* care. And he wanted to hear her answer.

"It's not as if you will be there with me."

He smiled faintly. Her cheeks were fiery red, but her husky voice was as tart as vinegar. "Then we have no problem. You take the bed. I'll make do. Elsewhere."

She blinked. "You were teasing me."

"Maybe a little," he allowed. Better that she think that. "My intentions are honorable." Sort of. "I've already moved some of my stuff out. Put on clean sheets. There's an attached bathroom with a shower that almost works. Clean towels and all."

Her cheeks reddened all over again. Charming him. Making him feel a hair guilty for involving her in his plan. Just because every time Darby looked at him with that energy that seemed to crackle about her, and every time she opened her mouth to speak in that husky, rich voice, making his brain short-circuit and turn from the business at hand to hot afternoons, tangled sheets and throaty moans didn't mean he couldn't control himself. He'd hired Darby to do a job. She would be well compensated. Double her normal pay.

Speaking of which—

"I'll also give you a check up front for your time," he said. He'd bet his antique tool collection that Darby's conscience would never let her run out on a job that she'd already been paid for.

"Actually, I'd prefer cash. If that's all right." She stood and brushed her hands down her shirt, then moved to the fireplace, studying the framed photos that sat on the plain mantel. "I'm not trying to avoid taxes or anything," she assured. "I just don't have a bank account."

"Don't trust bankers?"

She plucked one photo off the mantel. Her shoulder lifted casually. "What can I say? I'm strictly a money-in-the-mattress kind of girl."

Right. It was no skin off his nose how she preferred to be paid. "Cash it is, then. I'll have Carmel take care of it in the morning. I'll be gone all day tomorrow, so if you need anything you can call her at the office. She can track me down, though I doubt there's anything you'll need me for, anyway. I'll make sure to leave the numbers for you."

She smiled at him, but it was quick and nervous. Then she changed the subject. "This is a nice photograph of the falls."

Apparently, she still wasn't too anxious to take over his bed. He looked at the framed photo in her hand. "Is it? They all came with the place." He certainly made no claim to the pictures. Not the ones on the mantel or those hanging on the walls. The house had come furnished, right down to the ugly pink vases with the faded silk flower bouquets that bracketed the mantel.

"Georgie once mentioned that there is a legend surrounding the waterfall, but she didn't tell me what it was. Do you know?"

He knew. He just didn't believe. "That when two people discover love while looking at the falls, they'll have that love for a lifetime and beyond. Bull, if you ask me."

She nibbled her lip and set down the photo. "Did you, um, get all this stuff from your sister's house, too? Along with the cribs?" She touched her hand to a wind-up swing and set it in motion. "It's amazing how much stuff you need for children."

He nodded. The room was littered with enough baby equipment and toys to stock a children's boutique. "It would have been easier to move into Elise's place, but apparently Caldwell owns it. He's already put it on the market. Carmel managed to get this stuff out of the house before he sold all of *it,* too." Or moved it to his stone mansion on the hill in preparation for the grandchildren he was probably certain he'd be able to take away from Garrett.

Darby latched on to yet another topic. Almost desperately. "Your secretary seems very nice."

"Assistant. And she is nice. Worth twice her pay, but don't tell her I said that."

"Does she have children?"

"No."

"Mmm." Finally Darby seemed to run out of questions to ask, inane topics to broach. "Well. I guess I'll go to…go on up. Stairs. Now."

He stood and pretended that he didn't see her nearly jump out of her cute white tennis shoes. "I'll take your bag up for you.'' It was still where she'd left it in the kitchen.

''No!'' She darted in front of him and snatched up the long strap, practically yanking it out of his hand. ''Don't be silly. It's not heavy.''

He looked down at her. ''You're an intriguing mixture, Darby White,'' he murmured. A natural with the children. A woman with a voluptuous voice that sent shivers down his back.

''There's nothing intriguing about me.'' She slid past him. ''I'm just a…regular woman. Nothing special.'' Her voice whispered down the stairs as she lightly ran up. ''Good night.''

Garrett slowly reached out and turned off the lamp, plunging the room into darkness. He heard the soft thump of a door closing. Even though the house was silent, he knew it wasn't empty. It was an odd feeling.

Whether it was the presence of children he'd chosen to take responsibility for, or the presence of a woman who seemed panicked at the idea of spending the night under the same roof as a man, Garrett couldn't say.

The longer he thought about it, the more he was certain he was better off not knowing the answer.

Finally he went into the den. But instead of pulling out the sofa bed, he sat down at the desk and the pile of work waiting for him. He'd returned to Fisher Falls for one specific purpose.

Taking in his sister's children hadn't changed that in the least.

Chapter Five

Intriguing. The word kept hovering in Darby's mind. Annoying her.

She shook out a miniature-size T-shirt, folded it in two and added it to the growing stack on the kitchen table. Between three nine-month-olds and Reid and Regan, Darby had lost count of how many loads of wash she'd done in the past few days.

She didn't mind, though. Doing laundry was something that an ''ordinary'' woman would take care of. Cutting peanut butter and jelly sandwiches into cute triangles and strips was something an ''ordinary'' woman would do. An ''intriguing'' woman would not do those things.

Darby certainly hadn't done any of those things. Not even the last time she'd gotten entangled with a man and his winsome children. Bryan had had a host of servants and—

She pushed away the thought as she heard the distinctive jingle of keys in the front door. She finished folding the last shirt and stowed the laundry basket in the small laundry room and came out just as Garrett walked into the kitchen.

He dropped several long, cardboard tubes on the table. "Thought you'd be in bed by now."

She picked up the stack of laundry, catching one of the tubes as it began rolling off the table. *Good evening to you, too,* she thought. "I need to talk to you. You haven't been around much." Talk about an understatement. The man had practically vanished after the first evening Darby had arrived. He obviously worked killing hours, whether it was the weekend or not.

"I'm here now."

Even though she'd spent hours, days, building up a nicely steaming need to resolve a few things with this man, the words she'd thought, rehearsed, planned, stuck in her throat. It was the jeans he was wearing, she decided. Jeans and a gray T-shirt that clung to his chest and shoulders in an unsettling way. Up to now she'd only seen him wearing dress shirts, loosened ties and well-cut dark suits.

"You want me to guess what's on your mind?" Garrett asked after a moment. "Kids doing okay?"

She nodded. He hadn't shaved, either, she noticed. And he had a dingy piece of gauze bandage wrapped around one of his fingers.

"Nobody sick?"

"No." Her hands curled at her side. So what if he looked big and tough and tired and had a bandage that was positively raggedy? She'd never seen the appeal in whisker-bristled men, and he was certainly big enough to get himself a clean bandage for his banged finger.

"Well, actually, Tad's been running a bit of a temp," she admitted. "He's cutting another tooth. They're all asleep, now. I hope you don't mind, but I took them with me earlier today to visit Georgie."

"How's she doing?"

"She has good days and bad. She definitely enjoyed seeing the children. They had fun exploring the house. She has a ballroom. It's fairly empty, and we just let the triplets loose in there. Bridget's crawling more. And Keely's standing all on her own."

Garrett looked completely uninterested.

"Well, anyway. They've been asleep for hours now."

"That's good. Isn't it?" He looked at the kitchen window. The dark kitchen window. "It *is* late," he offered.

She ignored the way his eyes crinkled at the corners. His amusement wasn't appealing. "Exactly. It is late. Tomorrow is Sunday."

"Okay."

Her fingernails were poking into her palms. She unclenched her hands. "What arrangements have you made?"

Since the night of her arrival, Darby had talked more with Garrett's assistant than she had with him. But if Carmel knew anything about Garrett's long-range plans beyond the hearing—looming ever closer as Wednesday approached—she wasn't admitting it.

"Getting anxious to leave?"

"I'm concerned about the children," she said carefully.

"Aren't we all," he muttered. "The custody hearing will be here soon enough. If Caldwell has his way, I won't need a nanny at all.''

"So you *haven't* made other arrangements, yet.''

He looked at her. "Have you eaten? Of course you have,'' he answered himself. He walked around Darby and pulled open the refrigerator door.

She knew what he saw. She'd finally made arrangements with the nearby grocer to make a delivery that morning when it was obvious that Garrett wasn't going to do so himself. The refrigerator and cupboards were now well stocked. With the tip she'd added on, the arrangement had only gouged into half of the cash Carmel had delivered to Darby just as Garrett had promised.

Hiring someone to fix the air-conditioning had taken the other half of her pay. But her pay, or lack of it, wasn't really an issue she cared to get into. Garrett was obviously not made of money—as evidenced by his modest living conditions—even though he'd been generous about her pay.

He pulled out a can of cola and turned to face her as he popped the top and lifted it to his mouth. She looked away as he drank, his long, strong throat working.

Then he finally lowered the can and sighed. "No. I haven't made other arrangements.''

"But we agreed that I would help you out for only this week.''

"I didn't say I haven't *tried* to make other arrangements.'' He finished off the soda and crumpled the can with one hand. "The same problems still exist that existed last week, Darby. You're my only option. And even if you weren't,'' he added firmly, "you're my best option. The children adore you. How can you walk away from them?''

"How can *you* ignore them the way you have been?'' The words escaped without thought and she pressed her lips together. She was only the hired help, she reminded herself. *Temporary* hired help. She'd grown up with "help" all around her, and she knew that there were times when her father considered their input acceptable and times when he hadn't. "I'm sorry. I shouldn't have said that.''

He pulled out a chair and sat down, legs stretching halfway across the cozy kitchen. "Don't stand there like that,'' he said. "You remind me of the nuns from my elementary school. Except you're missing the ruler to rap over my knuckles.''

She reluctantly pulled out the chair opposite him and sat. With one hand, he rolled one of the long tubes a few inches back and forth across the table. That dirty bandage of his was going to drive her nuts. "I don't believe you ever went to parochial school,'' she finally said stiffly.

He shrugged. "You'll hear the rumors sooner or later. I wasn't exactly a teacher's pet. I told you before, Darby. People aren't jumping out of the woodwork to help me out. They're too afraid of upsetting The Mighty Caldwell.''

"Laura isn't afraid,'' Darby countered. "If she had been, she wouldn't have listened to anything I had to say about Elise's wishes. I think you may be exaggerating your—'' she hesitated when his eyebrow peaked, then plunged on "—your difficulties somewhat. I've found this town very welcoming. And if you just give people a chance, instead of assuming the worst, you'll be surprised. Nobody here is going to want you to fail with the children.''

He watched her from beneath lazy lids. Then he sat up straighter in his chair and propped his arms on the table, cocking his head to the side. ''Are you for real?''

Darby swallowed and leaned back an inch—all that the ladder-back chair allowed. ''I just think—''

''You'll see Wednesday at the hearing what kind of assumptions I've been making or not making,'' he said blandly. ''In fact, once Caldwell finds out that you've been helping me these last few days, you're not going to be on his Christmas list anymore, either.''

''I'm not afraid of your father.'' What she *did* fear was walking into that courtroom on Wednesday. She just hadn't figured a way of getting out of it.

He lifted one hand. ''Call him Mayor or Caldwell or Sir Snake,'' he suggested. ''But don't call him my father.'' His eyes narrowed. ''He hasn't called here, or been by, has he?''

''No.'' Which, when she thought about it, surprised her a little. The children *were* his grandchildren.

''Good. You don't need to be afraid of him, even if he does. I'll protect you from him. Just continue taking care of the kids. I'll make it worthwhile. Despite the looks of this place, I can afford whatever you ask.''

She shook her head, wondering where the conversation had gone amiss. ''You're as bad as Dane,'' she murmured wonderingly.

''Who's Dane?''

Her lips parted. ''I...nobody.'' How could she be so careless? She brushed back her bangs and stood. ''I can heat up some supper for you,'' she offered. ''We had fried chicken. There's still some left.''

Garrett caught her hand as she moved past him, nervous energy seeming to pour from her pores. He ran his thumb over the back of her smooth hand. It was slender and long-fingered. Elegant, he thought. ''Nobody?''

''Garrett, please.'' She tugged at her hand, but he didn't let go.

''I know why I'm edgy,'' he said. ''And I can understand why you might be annoyed with me about not making other arrangements for the fearsome five, but you're about ready to jump out of your skin. Who is Dane?''

He didn't know why he was making a big deal about it. If she had a secret or two, who was he to begrudge her of them? He had a whopper of one, himself. And because he did, his conscience needed to know that he was at least giving the kids a caretaker whom they actually liked. One who would stick around awhile. Not be lured off by some guy named *Dane.*

Darby's face was pale. ''My brother,'' she finally said stiffly.

Surprised, Garrett let her go. She wrapped the hand he'd held in her other, rubbing it. He frowned. He hadn't held her that tightly. ''Why didn't you just say so?''

''I…we don't get along,'' Darby said, turning away. ''Do you want that chicken or not?'' She took a plate out of the cupboard, and Garrett saw that her hand was trembling.

Hell.

He rose and put his hands around her shoulders,

gently turning her to face him. The sight of her glistening eyes grabbed his gut and twisted hard. He took the plate from her and set it aside. "Hey. I'm sorry. Don't do that."

She blinked and averted her face.

He caught her chin and gently lifted. "I know all about family feuds," he murmured. She looked up at him with those sky-blue eyes, and he clamped down on the heat that suddenly churned inside him. *That* was the last damned thing they needed.

Then she moistened her lips. Just a nervous, barely noticeable movement, and her soft lower lip glistened.

Ah, hell.

He drew his thumb over her chin. The hint of stubbornness in it saved her face from being perfectly oval. He could feel her pulse beating in her throat; rippling little beats that teased the heavy chug of his own pulse.

"Garrett." She pressed her palms flat against his shirt, and he could have sworn that he felt the distinct shape of each one of those long, elegant fingers.

"Shh." His thumb drifted over her lips and her eyes fluttered closed.

Beneath his thumb he felt her lips move. "I don't know which is worse," she whispered. "When you're all cold and distant or when you're...not."

"I told you to shush," he muttered. "Your voice. It's—"

"Rough," she finished.

"Husky," he corrected. Like a brush of velvet over his nerve endings.

She suddenly stepped back, looking anywhere but at him. Her fingertips touched her throat for a moment before she picked up the plate and held it in front of her like a shield. "My vocal chords were, um, injured when I was a kid. I know. I sound like a habitual smoker or something.''

It was good she'd backed away. She had more sense than he did. ''You sound like you,'' he said. But listening to her talk was an exercise in erotic torture. She said his name, and he nearly lost the ability to reason. And the kitchen still seemed filled with tension.

Tension that he'd caused because he'd let himself forget, for just a minute, that he needed more from this woman than the taste of her lips. He needed Darby for the kids. Without her in his corner, he knew his chances in court against Caldwell were slim. It was only her word, after all, that Elise had wanted him to take her and Marc's children. His attorney, Hayden Southerland, who had finally arrived from New Mexico, had confirmed it.

Actually what Hayden had said was that the only thing better than an unimpeachable nanny would be an unimpeachable wife. Since Garrett had no prospects on that score, he'd better remember to keep his hands off the one nanny he had in the offing here in Fisher Falls.

Once he got back home to Albuquerque, he'd see about hiring one of Carmel's aunts; she seemed to have about twenty of 'em. They were all devoted to their grandbabies but Garrett figured once he was back home, he could convince at least one of them that it would be worth their while to watch a few more.

He gathered up the tubes of blueprints from the table. ''Don't worry about the chicken,'' he told Darby. ''I've got work to do, anyway.'' Carrying the plans, he headed out of the kitchen for the den.

Just exactly like Dane, Darby thought, watching

him go. Her brother would work 24-7 if he could, and it seemed that Garrett would, too.

She quietly prepared a plate, heating the chicken in the microwave before adding a gelatin salad and a buttered roll. Garrett didn't particularly look the type to eat orange gelatin with bananas inside it, but Regan had helped Darby make it that afternoon, so that's what he would get. She poured a glass of milk, prepared everything on a tray and carried it, along with the small first aid kit from beneath the kitchen sink, to Garrett's den, turning off lights as she went.

He hadn't exaggerated about the work, she realized when she stepped inside the small room. He'd unrolled some blueprints across his desk and was thoroughly focused on them. She set the tray on the small table next to the couch that he was supposedly unfolding into a bed each night. Frankly, she didn't see how he could. The room was simply too cramped.

"Let me see that bandage." She flipped open the first aid kit on his desk and held out her hand.

He looked at his hand, as if surprised to see the sloppy bandage still circling his finger. "It's nothing."

"The bandage is dirty. Whatever you've done, you wouldn't want it to get infected, would you?" She wriggled her fingers, demanding.

His expression unreadable, he held up his hand and she unwrapped the tape and gauze, making a face at the cut beneath. "I thought you told people what to do at that construction company you run, not that you were out pounding nails with your own bare hands."

"Wasn't a nail." He didn't flinch as she cleansed the cut. "I was helping to install a window. It dropped. Made a helluva mess."

"Made a pretty good cut, too," she murmured.

"You know you probably should have had a stitch or two." She closed the edges with a butterfly bandage, then topped it with a cushy sterile pad.

"I was too busy getting on the horn to order another window. It was a custom job. It'll take weeks to get another."

"Figures you'd be more concerned with some window than your own health."

"It's just a cut, Darby."

"Cuts can get infected," she said smoothly. "Keep it covered." She pressed the last bit of tape into place and gathered up the old bandage and the wrappings from the new one and left the room.

She put the first aid kit back in the kitchen, then went upstairs. In the second bedroom, she picked up Regan's stuffed bear and tucked it back in bed with her. Reid had kicked off his blanket and Darby's hand hovered over the edge of it, but she didn't move it for fear that he'd wake. He slept so uneasily, poor sweetheart.

Finally Darby let him be. It wasn't cold in the house, after all. She went into the master bedroom and checked the triplets. Tad's face still felt a little warm to her, but he slept as soundly as Bridget and Keely.

She gathered up her nightshirt and her little bag of toiletries and went to use the bathroom downstairs. She didn't want to wake up the children by using the ensuite. As she crept down the dark stairs, she could see the light shining in Garrett's den, could hear the low murmur of his voice. He was talking on the phone.

Good, she thought as she closed herself in the bathroom and turned on the light. That meant he'd be busy long enough for her to get ready for bed, then scoot back upstairs through the dark, with him none the wiser. This was the first evening he was home early enough for her to even *feel* awkward about showering downstairs. She flipped on the shower, letting it warm while she cleaned her face and brushed her teeth. Then she showered and dried off in record time, gathered up her stuff and opened the door.

"The air conditioner is working again."

Darby gasped and jumped back, hitting the wall behind her. The bundle of clothes, towel and toiletries tumbled out of her grasp, and she glared at Garrett's shape in the dark hallway. "I had it fixed. And you scared me to death!" She went down on her knees, hands searching in the dark for her things. She found her clothes, at least.

Light suddenly flooded the narrow hallway and she looked up to see him standing over her, his long fingers and pristine bandage still resting against the wall switch. "Need help?" he asked smoothly.

She flushed and looked back down, snatching up the bits of ivory silk that passed for bra and panties and burying them along with her shirt and shorts inside her damp bath towel. She reached forward and plucked the toiletry bag from where it rested against the toe of his scuffed work boot. "No, I don't need help." She stood and wished the light wasn't quite so bright there in the hall. Her oatmeal-colored nightshirt hung to her knees, but she still felt exposed.

Definitely not a good thing after that crazy episode in the kitchen. He wasn't her type, and she wasn't his. And even if they were, it was still out of the question. She was only here to help with the children. She owed them that, at least.

"Why aren't you using one of the baths upstairs?"

"I didn't want to wake the children." She began

inching her way along the hall. "The pipes for both showers up there rattle really badly, and the water pressure is terrible. I'm sorry if I disturbed you." The stairs were nearly behind her now.

His lips twisted. "Too late for that. Who fixed the AC?"

"The guy Georgie uses." The toiletry bag fell off the stack in her arms again as she started up the stairs.

Before she could reach it, Garrett bent and picked it up. "Did he leave a bill?"

"I paid him when he came." She reached out for the bag. Standing on the second riser, they were nearly eye to eye. "Could I have that back, please?"

"I was planning to fix it myself."

"Well, now you don't have to. My bag?"

"How much was it?"

"Five ninety-five."

His eyebrows rose. "To fix the thermostat? Darby, he's a crook. Give me his name and I'll straighten him out."

"For the bag," Darby said sweetly. "Five dollars and ninety-five cents. On sale at the discount store as I recall. And I'd like it back. Unless you're wanting to borrow my razor because your own is dull?"

That stubble-shadowed jaw cocked. "How much was the repair bill, Darby?" She told him and still he didn't hand back her little bag. "I'll reimburse you," he said.

She wasn't going to argue about it. Despite her suspicion that he really wasn't as flush financially as he assured her, it wasn't as if she, herself, still had unlimited resources at her fingertips. "Fine."

He looked over her head. "I'm sorry the pipes are

so bad. When it was just me here, it was no big deal. I'll see what I can do about fixing it."

She lifted her shoulder, feeling uncomfortable. "After Wednesday, it won't make any difference to me," she reminded and promptly felt like a shrew for doing so. "I'm sorry. That sounded harsh."

"It sounded honest," he said evenly. "Good night, Darby."

She watched him walk back into the den where he closed the door. She blew out a breath and trudged up the stairs to the room she shared with the triplets. *Brilliantly handled, Darby.*

She hung the towel in the bathroom and checked Tad's forehead once more before sitting on the far side of the enormous bed. She pulled a clean outfit from the small chest situated beside the bed and the wall and set it out for the morning, but didn't close the drawer. Under the neatly rolled socks and undies, she could see the edge of the magazine she'd brought.

It was stupid to carry it with her, of course. There was no need. Every word was etched in her memory.

Yet she took it with her wherever she went. A talisman? A warning reminder?

Still, Darby pulled the slick, colorful periodical from beneath her clothing. It was two years old and easily fell open to the article. On one page was a collage of photographs. Some were old black-and-whites. Most were more recent. Fuzzy distance shots, painfully clear close-ups.

Sighing a little, Darby sat back against the pillows. There was Dane when he'd finally been promoted to president of the company. She ran her fingertip along the image of his face. Seven years her senior, he was impossible and overbearing. And she didn't like admitting that she missed him even the slightest little bit.

But she did.

For a long time they'd been a team. Until he took his place alongside their father, and Darby had once again been alone.

She turned the page to another set of photos. Her graduation. The front of the Schute Clinic in Kentucky where she'd had her first nursing job. The formal engagement photograph. The caption—Intriguing Debra White Rutherford To Wed Media Mogul Heir Bryan Augustine. Only there had been no marriage. No happily ever after. Only a year-long engagement that ended in humiliation.

One of the triplets snuffled, and Darby looked over at the cribs. She knew why she was looking at the magazine. Looking at the chronicle of her family's life; each memory a stabbing little wound.

In the kitchen with Garrett, breathing in his warm scent, feeling his heartbeat beneath his gray shirt, she'd forgotten. For a moment. And she couldn't afford to ever forget. Now, since the accident with Garrett's sister, she didn't deserve to forget.

She climbed off the bed, shoving the magazine back in its hiding place beneath her socks and went over to the cribs. She looked down at the sweetly scented babies. "I'm sorry," she whispered. "If I could undo it all, I would."

They slept on.

And Darby snapped off the small table lamp and forced herself to climb into the bed that belonged to the man downstairs. She only wished she could close off thoughts of that man as easily as she'd closed the drawer on the magazine.

Instead, she lay there, wakeful for a long while. Staring into the dark, trying to convince herself that the pillow beneath her head didn't smell wonderfully of Garrett.

Chapter Six

"**I**'m hungry."

Garrett lowered the newspaper he was reading to the kitchen table and looked at his niece. Her hair stuck out in tangles and the pink-striped sundress she wore looked as if it was on backward. It was only seven in the morning. "Do you want a bagel?" He held up his own.

She shook her head and he set the bagel half back on his plate. "What *do* you want, Regan?" He wasn't going to play guessing games when it came to food with her. He'd done that too many times before Darby had come to stay, and he wasn't falling for it again.

"Waffles."

"Then you'll have to wait for Darby to get up so she can fix them for you," he told her. "I don't do waffles."

She sniffed, and she was so much like Elise had

been—all snooty and regal—that he felt irritation rise. He jabbed his fingers through his hair and focused on his niece, reminding himself to be patient. She was only four, and her world had violently changed only a week ago. "I can heat up a frozen waffle," he offered.

"Frozen waffles aren't *real* waffles," she said.

He shrugged. He wasn't going to take offense at a comment from a four-year-old waffle connoisseur. "Then you'll have to wait for Darby. Where is Reid?" He leaned over to the counter and snagged the coffeepot to refill his mug.

Regan scooted out a chair and climbed up on it, sitting high on her knees and leaning over the edge of the table, anchoring his newspaper with her elbows. "I dunno. I don't like you."

"Why?"

Her eyebrows drew together. She poked at the edge of the newspaper with her fingertip, deliberately tearing it. "'Cause you're mean."

Garrett looked at her over his coffee. "And you're rude," he returned smoothly.

"No, I'm not. I'm a princess. My mommy told me so."

"I'm sure she did. But even princesses have good manners."

"They certainly do," Darby commented from the doorway. She held out her hand for Regan. "Apologize to your uncle Garrett for what you said. "

"She doesn't have to apologize for telling me what she thinks," Garrett said. He held up the page of the newspaper that was ripped crookedly through the article he'd been reading. "You can apologize for doing this," he told Regan.

She pouted. "It was a accident."

"You can still be sorry for an accident," Darby said. "Excuse us." She didn't look at Garrett as she led the girl out of the room.

He could hear them talking, then the temper-filled stomp of small feet going upstairs. Darby returned and headed for the coffee. She poured a cup and held it to her face, inhaling deeply. "Nectar of the gods," she murmured.

He dragged his attention from her legs. But it wasn't easy. Not with the thigh-length white sundress she wore. "Is Regan upstairs making a voodoo doll of me to stick pins into?"

"No. She's just testing you, Garrett. To see where the boundaries are."

"I'm not a complete idiot."

Her lips parted. "I...know that." She set aside her coffee cup and pulled a carton of eggs out of the fridge. "I expected you to be at work by now."

"Disappointed?"

She whirled around, and he smiled faintly. Rolling her eyes, she turned back to what she was doing.

"I thought I'd take a crack at the plumbing," he admitted. "The office won't fall apart without me for a few hours."

She was cracking eggs into a pan. "Why don't you just hire someone? The owner should take care of it, anyway, just like all the other things wrong around here."

"They should, but they haven't. And I'm a hands-on guy, what can I say? Do you always wear white or tan-colored clothes?"

Her movements slowed for only a moment. "Yes. I'm a bland kind of girl. What can I say?"

"Hardly bland. More like a refreshing vanilla ice cream on a hot summer day."

Her eyes were amused. "My, my. Poetry. What are you angling for now? Another 'barely a week' of child care?"

He shook out his paper and started reading again. There was another article about the accident. This time, instead of the usual focus about Elise's family connections, the subject of the article was the other driver, who'd apparently had some pretty serious connections himself. To the kind of wealth and power that Caldwell could only dream.

"Just saying what I think. Like Regan does. Did you see this article? That Phil Candela guy was apparently some mucky-muck with Rutherford Transportation outta Kentucky. Wonder what he was doing in Fisher Falls."

"Maybe he was on his way through to somewhere else," she said abruptly. "What are you really doing here? Why aren't you out conquering the world of construction?"

"Fixing the plumbing," he assured. His coffee mug was empty again and he stood, reaching for the pot. What he was really doing was trying to follow Hayden's suggestion that, if he wanted to win in court against Caldwell, he needed to show at least some makings of a family man.

"Want more?" He held up the pot. She shook her head, and he realized her cup was still brimming full. "Still too hot to drink?"

"Oh, I don't drink the stuff. Tastes horrid. I just like the smell."

"Sacrilege," he grumbled, pouring the rest of the pot into his cup. "Heresy."

"Good taste." She slid two fried eggs onto a plate and handed them to him, shutting off the stove in the same motion. "Eat your eggs. I'm going to get the kids now, so if you don't want to get in the way of flying food, you'll eat them quickly and escape."

He took the plate. "Darby." She paused in the doorway, looking back at him. "About last night. In here."

Her skin turned pink. "It was late," she dismissed.

He hadn't quite known what he'd been going to say. But he knew it wasn't that. "Yeah, right," he said blandly. "Late."

Four hours later he was cursing the idiot who'd installed the pipes, the idiot inspector who'd approved them and the idiot corporation that owned the house and probably a dozen others just like it. He'd hunched into crawlspaces, climbed through the sloppily insulated attic, torn out a good piece of wall and dug a ditch near the foundation deep enough to swim in.

"Having fun?"

He looked up at Darby from hosing off his muddy hands. She'd brought the kids out to the backyard and they'd all been chasing a bright beach ball around the grass. In fact, Darby had several grass stains on her sundress, which wasn't a dress at all, he'd realized. The skirt of her dress was actually shorts, as he'd seen when she'd been trying to teach Regan how to turn cartwheels.

She seemed almost driven to show the kids a fun time.

"There's a leak that could sink a ship," he muttered.

"No ship could sink in this much mud." She gestured toward his jeans. Mud caked them up to the knees. "The children have been begging to play in it like their uncle Garrett has been."

"Hell, yeah. It'll be one big game to replace the entire section of pipe from the main to the house."

The ball bounced their way, and Darby caught it, laughing when her bare foot slipped in the mud. She barely caught herself from falling on her rear. "You said you were a hands-on guy. If you don't want to fix it yourself, hire someone. You run a construction company, for heaven's sake!" She tossed the ball at him and it bounced off his chin before he dropped the hose and caught it in his muddy hands.

Actually, he owned the construction company, but he didn't correct her. He tossed the ball back at her, and it left a muddy mark against her white outfit, right over the enticing thrust of her breasts. She stared down at herself, her expression surprised. Then her lashes lowered.

His eyes narrowed at the sly look she cast him. Suddenly she struck, reaching the hose just before he did, and turning it full on in his face.

Ignoring the streaming water, he hooked his arm around her waist and tipped her off her feet, holding her easily over the mud bath below them.

"No, no, wait," she gasped, giggling so hard her face was red. "I'm sorry. Really. That was…was completely inappropriate of me."

He squinted through the water she was still squirting in his face. "Inappropriate?" He finally managed to redirect the hose. Right at her. "I'll show you inappropriate."

She shrieked and wriggled, her hands pushing at him.

Garrett laughed. And it struck him then that it had been a long time since he'd done so. Water soaked his shirt, soaked her clothes. The children were watching them, agog. He laughed so hard his chest hurt.

He laughed so hard, his hold on Darby loosened. She twisted free, her feet tangling with his legs, and down they went.

Mud splattered.

Water gushed.

"I can't believe you did this!" Darby tried to sit up and ended up only spreading more mud. She planted her hands on Garrett's chest for traction.

"Me? I didn't trip us," he pointed out. He was sprawled on his back, half in the muddy trench, half on the grass. There were streaks of mud on his cheek. "Besides, you started it all with the bouncing ball."

He lifted his head to look at her. "You know, I don't think I've laughed in this town since I was five years old."

Darby's throat tightened. She realized her hands were still pressed against his chest. It might as well have been bare for all the protection his soaking-wet T-shirt provided. "I didn't laugh a whole lot in my childhood, either," she admitted.

"You need a bath." Regan stood beside them, her nose wrinkled.

Darby chuckled. "You've certainly got that right, peaches."

"I'm not a peach. I'm a princess."

Garrett reached out and dashed his fingertip across her nose, leaving a streak of mud. "A princess with mud on her nose."

Reid ran up beside his sister, sticking out his face. "Do me. Do me."

Darby watched Regan's expression. The little girl didn't know whether to laugh or be insulted. But when Reid giggled wildly at the dollop of mud Garrett deposited on his button nose, she finally grinned. She crouched down and gathered up a handful of the slick stuff and turned on her heel, running toward the triplets who were corralled in the playpen.

Darby groaned. "Too much of a good thing," she decided quickly and scrambled to her feet. She caught up to Regan and redirected the girl. In minutes Regan and Reid were making mud pies, and the toddlers had escaped their own "anointing."

She had muddy handprints all over her dress, and her legs and feet were coated. Garrett was hosing himself off again. She started across the yard toward him, stopping short when he suddenly yanked off his shirt and dropped it on the ground beside him before turning the hose over his head like a shower.

Regan tugged on her shorts, and Darby dragged her gaze from the sight of water streaming off Garrett's broad shoulders.

"Uncle Garrett's getting naked."

"No, sweetheart." Her voice felt strangled. "He just took off his shirt because he's all muddy from working on the plumbing. See? He's just cleaning up a little." She couldn't keep from looking back at him and felt her stomach jolt at the sight.

She brushed her wet hair back from her face and focused on the much safer sight of her miniature charges. "While you guys are making mud desserts there, I'm going to make our main course. We'll eat out here. Have a picnic. Sound good?"

Enthusiastic cheers followed her as she walked toward Garrett. He'd turned the hose on an assortment of tools. "Mind if I use the hose there for a little rinsing myself?"

He pointed the hose at her legs, and she shivered a little as the cold water washed away the mud. But it was a good shiver because the day was almost unbearably hot. "So, are you going to be able to fix the leak you found?"

He didn't look at her as he nodded, and Darby stifled a sigh. For a while there he'd laughed. The sound had delighted her just as much as when she'd heard Regan and Reid giggling in the bathroom that first night.

Now, however, he'd apparently put his sense of humor back on ice.

"I'm going to fix some lunch. Would you like some?"

"No. I'm gonna pick up some materials to get this mess taken care of." He bent over, hooking his fingers through the handle of his red toolbox.

Darby folded her arms, looking anywhere but at the play of muscles across his smooth, hard back. You'd think she'd never seen a male torso before.

You haven't. Not one like this.

She ignored the voice. "You've got to eat," she said to him.

"I'll grab something while I'm gone." He straightened, hefting the heavy box with ease.

"But—"

"Darby." His jaw looked tight. "Let me take care of the plumbing and my stomach, and you take care of the five minis. Deal?"

She frowned, glancing at the children. They were perfectly occupied in the yard. Safely fenced in. The only dangers were squishy, messy mud and grass stains. She followed Garrett around the side of the house, latching the gate behind her. "Have I upset you? I know I'm just the nanny and you're the boss, but it was just so funny. I couldn't resist."

"Some things I can't resist, either," he said roughly. "And dammit, Darby, you're soaking wet."

She ran her hands through her wet hair. "So are you."

"I'm not wearing white." He ran his finger along the narrow strap over her shoulder. "You are."

She flushed, hastily crossing her arms over her chest. "I didn't realize."

"I did."

"I'm sorry."

Garrett exhaled in a thin stream and stepped in her path when she turned to go. "I'm not. But that's a problem I'm just gonna have to deal with."

Her chin angled. "There's no problem. I wasn't throwing myself at you."

"No, you were throwing mud and—"

"I said I was sorry."

"You were throwing smiles and laughter, too. And the kids loved it. So stop apologizing."

Her mouth closed. But only for a moment. "Is the water turned back on inside the house, then?"

"Yeah."

"Good. Well. Okay, then. Be sure you put a fresh bandage on your finger."

He'd told himself he wouldn't. "I loved it, too," he admitted. And sliding his hand around her neck, he pulled her to him and pressed his mouth to hers.

He heard her squeak. Felt her gasp. Tasted her shock. Her surprise.

Her hands touched his arms. Rose to his shoulders.

Destroyed his intentions. His toolbox hit the ground with a heavy thud.

He slid one arm around her narrow waist. It was like holding a fluttering wild thing against him. Like tasting an exotic, heady spice. He kissed her jaw. The pulse thundering frantically beneath her ear. "Open your mouth," he muttered.

She inhaled and he felt the thrust of her breasts against him. The heat that had been simmering inside him bubbled. He covered her mouth again, tasting. Going deeper, needing—

"Well, this is about what I expected of you."

The intrusive voice barely penetrated Garrett's brain. But Darby sprang back from him as if she'd been shot.

He shifted, shielding her behind him, and stared at the one man he could truly say he hated.

Caldwell Carson.

"I've never much been interested in what you expect," Garrett said evenly.

"Carrying on in plain sight of my grandchildren with one of your—"

"Don't say it," Garrett warned. "And they're *my* nieces and nephews. In case you've forgotten."

"I've forgotten nothing," Caldwell snapped. "Particularly the fact that Elise never had anything to do with you. This story you've managed to concoct may have convinced a few people for now, but it won't last."

Darby slid past Garrett's restraining arm, dismay darkening her bright eyes. "Mayor Carson, I know your loss has been terrible. But Elise did say—"

"Who are you?"

Garrett silenced her with a look. "Take the kids

inside," he ordered flatly. "And keep them there until he's gone."

She bit her lip, clearly reluctant. But finally she went, leaving Garrett alone with his father. "What are you doing here, Caldwell? Slumming?"

"I came to see my grandchildren. That secretary of yours has put me off long enough. You wouldn't take my calls, so here I am. I want to see them."

"Not today, Gramps."

"You can't keep them from me."

"I can as long as I'm their guardian."

"That'll end on Wednesday."

"So you keep threatening. Frankly, I'm pretty bored with it all."

"Do you have *no* respect for your sister at all?"

Cold anger settled inside him. "Have you? You slapped a For Sale sign on her house before anyone could blink. You were huddling with your lawyers before my *sister* was even buried." His lips twisted. "You never did have any respect for the dead."

"Your mother would be ashamed of you."

Garrett's hand curled. It took everything he possessed not to raise it. "The only shame in my mother's life was her involvement with you."

"I loved Bonnie."

"I'm sure your wife found that as comforting as the rest of us. You loved *women*," Garrett corrected flatly. "My mother was just one more to you." He stared at Caldwell, seeing the physical resemblance between himself and the older man and hating it. "No comment?"

"You can't keep those children from me," Caldwell finally said. His voice was harsh. "For God's sake, Son. They're all I have left."

Garrett knew that. How well he knew that, and how well he knew just how much like this cold old man he really was. "Don't call me Son."

Then he picked up his tool chest and walked away.

He stopped short at the sight of Darby standing inside the fence. The children were nowhere in sight.

"Garrett, I—" she hesitated "—are you all right?"

His jaw tightened until it ached. He wanted, needed, her on his side to win his case against Caldwell. But right now, the soft look in her eyes was more than he could take.

"I told you to go inside," he said flatly. But instead of having the desired effect, the look in her eyes softened even more before she turned and headed into the house.

Leaving him. Alone.

Chapter Seven

Thunder crashed overhead, sounding as if mountains were caving in on the house. Darby pressed her hands to her ears, wishing she could blot out the violent sounds of the electrical storm raging outside.

Another rumble. Starting far off in the distance, rolling closer and closer, building strength, plowing over Garrett's two-story rented house. Windows rattled. Glasses inside the cupboard rattled. The entire house seemed to rattle.

Darby shuddered and decided that sitting in the kitchen wasn't the place to be, after all.

She gathered up the newspapers that had been piling up on the counter and carried them, along with her iced tea, into the living room. It was odd, she thought, listening to the storm brewing while it was swelteringly hot outside. There just seemed to be something wrong with that picture.

Georgie had told her about the storms that seemed to shake the world with fury. All noise and no show, she'd said.

Frankly, Darby figured the noise was bad enough to give the unwary a heart attack.

She set the newspapers on the couch, peered into the playpen where Keely and Bridget were sleeping, sound as could be. She didn't know how it was possible to sleep while thunder shook the house, but she wasn't going to argue with it. Tad was gnawing half-heartedly on his frozen teething ring. Hopefully, he'd fall asleep, too.

Regan and Reid weren't seemingly bothered by the racket, either. The two blond heads barely looked up from the video they were watching over the coloring books Georgie had given them.

She sat down on the couch and flipped through the newspapers, hoping that she wouldn't see another article about Phil Candela's connection to Rutherford Transportation. So far, the newspaper had run several little blurbs about the man, including details of his funeral in Kentucky. Darby had sent flowers, but she'd been too cowardly to sign her name to them.

She bypassed articles about the increase of housing starts in Fisher Falls and the appointment of a new police chief, skimmed one about an upcoming carnival and lingered over a half-page advertisement of G&G Construction and Development, which was currently hiring in the area.

She flipped to the comic-strip section, which was more her usual focus and had been for years and years.

It was an old habit learned when she'd been only fifteen and the front pages were always containing some piece of news about her family. Her father was squiring around another starlet or heiress even as he inked the deal to acquire another small, struggling company. Her brother had won another race, received another award.

Every time there had been an article, Darby had found herself being approached by yet another person claiming to be her friend. A friend who wanted an introduction to her sexy older brother. A friend who wanted an invitation to their estate, just coincidentally when the governor and his wife were visiting for the weekend.

It had taken Darby a while to understand that *she* wasn't the appeal for these people, but when she'd finally learned, she'd learned it well.

Too bad she hadn't learned it before it was time to walk down the aisle with a groom who'd decided she wasn't worth her father's bribe after all.

Disgusted with the depressing thoughts, Darby pushed aside the papers and leaned into the playpen to pick up Tad. "You don't need a bribe to like me, do you, Tad?"

But instead of spitting out his teething ring and grinning at her the way he always did, he just looked at her with his brown eyes fever bright.

Darby's adrenaline kicked in. She propped him on her hip and carried him upstairs to take his temp. Something that he did not like at all.

And she didn't like at all the fact that it was so high. He was teething, but that didn't account for a temp this high.

She didn't even know any of the pediatricians in town. The only doctor with whom she'd had any dealings had been Georgie's physician.

Smiling into Tad's unhappy face, she maneuvered

him into shorts and a clean shirt and carried him back downstairs. He rested his hot face against her neck, his fingers tangling in her shirt.

"Regan, sweetie." She sat down on the coffee table where Regan and Reid were drawing. "Do you remember ever going to the doctor?"

Regan nodded. "For a shot." Her eyes slid to Reid. "He cried. But I didn't."

Reid pushed her arm. "Uh-huh," he argued. "You did too cry."

"Do you remember his name?"

"Who?"

"The doctor, Regan. What did you call the doctor when he gave you the shot?"

Her lips pursed. Then she shrugged and picked up another crayon. "I dunno."

Darby gave up on that tack. Another boom of thunder rocketed the windows, and Tad started to cry. She hugged him gently and searched out a phone book. There were three pediatricians in town, but when she called them, none had any of the Northrop children listed in their records.

She called Garrett, but reached only Carmel, who said she was on her way out the door to a meeting and Garrett was at one of their building sites. Growing more frustrated by the minute, Darby called Smiling Faces. The only medical information in the children's files was their parents' insurance policy number and a notarized form that said Smiling Faces could obtain medical care for the children in an emergency—two things that didn't help Darby in the least. Molly finally offered to send Beth over to watch the children while Darby took Tad to the hospital for a quick check.

It was about the least appealing solution Darby

could have imagined, but at least she wouldn't have to cart all five of them around in the brewing storm. When Beth finally arrived, Darby wanted to drag the young woman into the house and throttle her for taking so long. Instead, she gathered up Tad and hurried out to her car, fastening him into the car seat as she kept one eye on the angry-looking sky overhead. So far, Georgie's words had proved true. All noise.

Tad started crying again when her car backfired, and she tried singing to distract him. It didn't work and by the time she carried him into the emergency room at the hospital, she felt like crying herself.

Particularly when the admitting nurse refused to admit him without the guardian's approval. Darby leaned over the desk and stared the prune-faced woman in the face. Calmly explaining the situation had gotten her nowhere. "I want this child examined. Right now." There wasn't one other single person in the waiting room.

"Then find the child's guardian," the other woman retorted.

"I've told you. He's not available right now. For heaven's sake! This is the mayor's grandson," Darby gritted.

"I don't care if he's the president's grandson."

Darby hissed with annoyance. Carrying Tad on her hip, she walked right past the admitting desk, through the double doors, to the first exam room, ignoring the voluble protests following her. "You can't just go back there!"

"Watch me," Darby muttered. She pressed her lips to Tad's hot forehead, looking around until she found an otoscope. He'd been tugging at his ears, and she wasn't surprised to find them both red. Inflamed. She carried him back out to the admitting desk where a security officer had been summoned. "He needs an antibiotic," Darby said.

"Miss White, I don't know *who* you think you are, but—"

"What's going on here?"

Darby whirled on her heel, gaping at Garrett who was standing behind her. When he'd left the house, he'd been wearing a black suit. But now he was in worn-white jeans and a black T-shirt that hugged his chest and arms. She swallowed, determined not to think about how it had felt to be held against that wide, warm chest, and cuddled Tad. "You look as if you've been installing windows yourself again. When did you get here?"

"Just now. Carmel told me you were looking for me and when I called the house, someone named Beth told me you'd brought Tad here." His gaze flicked over the infuriated admitting nurse and the bored security guard. "So what's the deal?"

"Otitis—" she broke off at the sharpened look he gave her. "Ear infection," she finished. "I suspect. But they won't examine him without your permission."

"So I'm giving my permission now." Garrett raised his eyebrow at the nurse. "Well? Some reason why you're still sitting on your thumbs?"

The nurse rose, shoving a blank form toward them. "Give him to me."

Darby shook her head. Tad was clinging to her with a grip that was nearly painful, but even if he hadn't been, she wouldn't have surrendered the precious boy to this cranky woman. "I'll come with you."

They went into the same examining room. Two

minutes later, the doctor arrived and confirmed what Darby already knew. He wrote out a prescription and disappeared with a flap of his lab coat. Darby and Tad rejoined Garrett before he'd even finished completing the lengthy medical form.

"Ear infection," she said, handing the square of white paper to Garrett. "We need that filled right away." She carried Tad over to a molded plastic chair in the waiting room and sat down, holding him in her lap.

After several minutes Garrett walked their way, folding a pink sheet of paper and tucking it in the pocket of his jeans. "That nurse isn't real happy with you," he murmured as they left.

Darby sniffed. "That woman shouldn't even call herself a nurse. She didn't have one iota of compassion for Tad here. I'd be ashamed if I were her."

Thunder banged overhead, seeming to agree with her. Tad cringed. Darby shuddered. And Garrett grinned. "Don't like the percussion?"

"Not much." She tried to reach her purse, but couldn't. Not with the way Tad had his arms and legs wrapped around her. She gently detached him and handed him toward Garrett.

His grin faltered, then he took the tot, holding him awkwardly.

Tad howled.

Darby frowned at them both. "For heaven's sake, Garrett. Hold him next to you. He's probably afraid you're going to drop him like that." She rooted through her purse, found her keys, then dropped them again when another clap of thunder exploded around them.

"I think I'll drive to the pharmacy," Garrett suggested. He pushed Tad back into her arms and tugged her over to his truck. "We'll get your rust bucket later."

She knew she should be insulted, but she was too glad to climb into the safety of his big truck where the thunder overhead didn't seem to be quite so near. She fastened Tad into one of the built-in car seats the shiny new vehicle possessed, then Garrett drove out of the hospital's parking lot, heading to the drugstore that was just down the block.

He went inside and came out a short time later with a small white sack that he tossed into her lap. Darby didn't waste any time. She climbed into the back seat and gave Tad a dose of the sticky pink liquid right then and there.

Garrett watched her in the rearview mirror. Saw the way she tenderly smoothed Tad's wispy blond hair and tucked his soft little blanket against his cheek, murmuring sweet nothings under her breath as she tended to him.

Then she climbed back into the front seat and sighed deeply. Her fingertips drummed against her thigh, just below the hem of her toast-colored shorts. "I should've known he was getting sick. Garrett, I didn't even know who their pediatrician is. It wasn't even on record at Smiling Faces. You've got to get that information so this doesn't happen again."

He nodded. "I'll get whatever you need."

Her blue gaze settled on him. "It's not what *I* need. It's stuff that *you* need. As their guardian."

"Fine. I'll make sure I get it." He glanced in the mirror again at his nephew. "Is he going to be okay?"

"Sure. He'll be fine, as long as the antibiotic does

its work. He'll probably be feeling better within a few hours, actually.''

''That fast?''

''Children are pretty resilient.'' She looked out the window.

''Good. I wouldn't want Caldwell to go around saying tomorrow at the hearing that they were receiving inadequate care. He doesn't need any additional ammunition against me.''

''Not even the mayor could prevent ear infections,'' she murmured. ''Children just get them. Some more often than others.''

''You're good with them.'' He forced his attention away from the vulnerable curve of her neck, exposed by the scoop-necked shirt she wore and her feathery hair, and concentrated on negotiating the surprisingly busy rush-hour traffic. ''It's a wonder you don't have a passel of kids yourself already. You'll be a good mother.''

''No husband,'' she reminded him.

''Lack of a husband didn't stop my mother.'' He wished he'd kept his mouth shut as soon as the words were out.

''Yes, well, having parents who are married isn't always what it's cracked up to be, either.''

She looked as enthusiastic about her statement as he felt about his. Then another explosion of thunder rocked through the air and she leaned forward, looking up through the windshield at the sky. ''I can't believe it's not raining. Does it do this a lot?''

''Every year. You haven't been here that long?''

''Just a few months,'' she admitted.

''Where from?''

Her shoulder lifted. ''Everywhere. Nowhere.''

"And Georgina Vansant took you in."

"She's my…friend. I've known her a long time."

Garrett was certain that wasn't what Darby had been going to say. "She's a good woman. Fair. She offered me a job once. Way back when."

Her lips curved. "Really. Doing what?"

"Yard work." He smiled faintly, remembering. "She probably thought if I was busy enough trimming the hedges around her property I couldn't get into trouble elsewhere."

"Did you work for her, then?"

He shook his head, his smile dying. "Nope. Never even saw her house up close. My mother sent me to New Mexico to live with her cousin, instead."

"How did you like it there?"

He pulled into the driveway and parked. "I lived. Obviously. He was an ex-cop turned finish carpenter. He put me to work with him, mostly because he didn't trust me out of his sight at first."

"So that's how you got into construction?"

"Yeah."

"Well, it seems that has worked out fairly well for you."

He nodded and watched as she climbed into the back to release Tad's restraints, then carry him into the house. Garrett pocketed his keys and followed.

As soon as he entered the living room, Regan popped up and ran headlong into him, wrapping her arms around his leg as if he were her absolute favorite treat. He was so surprised he nearly jerked back. She smiled up at him, her brown eyes twinkling and her blond curls bouncing. "I drew you a picture," she announced.

Garrett gingerly unlatched her hands. "Uh, that's nice."

She skipped back to the coffee table and waved a piece of paper in the air. "See?"

Darby came down the steps just then. "That's beautiful, Regan. Why don't we put it on the refrigerator door so we can look at it every day."

Regan nodded and disappeared into the kitchen with Reid right on her heels.

Beth—Garrett remembered her now from the day he'd gone to Smiling Faces—was smiling at him. Her teeth were white and even and her white-blond hair flowed over shapely shoulders, curling just beneath a pair of breasts that gave new meaning to the short-sleeved pink sweater she wore.

She swayed over to Garrett, her long lashes fluttering. "You poor man," she pouted. "You must be just overwhelmed with everything that has happened."

"No."

His short answer didn't deter her. "I can't imagine how you're getting by." Flutter-flutter. "I was so glad that I could help you out today when you needed me."

"Darby needed you."

"That's right," Darby said from the kitchen doorway. "So thanks a lot, Beth." She crossed the carpet, holding out a folded bill. "That ought to cover your time, I think."

Beth's expression tightened a hair. "Don't be silly, Darby. I wouldn't dream of taking money for helping you out."

Darby's eyebrows rose. "Oh. I guess I misunderstood you then when you said it'd be ten dollars an hour."

Garrett swallowed a chuckle at the consternation on

Beth's face. "I'll be in the den," he said, and escaped while the escaping was good.

Darby continued holding out the cash. Beth snatched it out of her hand, her lips tight. "You didn't have to do this in front of *him,*" she hissed.

Darby shrugged. "Thanks for coming over. I do appreciate it." That was sincere, at least.

"When are you coming back to Smiling Faces?" Beth's eyes were fastened hungrily on the closed door to Garrett's den.

"If Garrett has his way, no time soon." She ought to feel ashamed for baiting Beth, but then Beth should be ashamed for the way she was practically throwing herself at Garrett.

And she didn't exactly appreciate the disbelieving look the other woman cast her way.

"Molly's not going to like that," Beth predicted. "You know, the only reason she hired you in the first place is because she's friends with Mrs. Vansant."

Since it was true, Darby couldn't very well argue the point. She started herding Beth to the door. "Whatever I end up doing, I'll work it out with Molly." She smiled. "Unless you've been promoted and are handling more than the check-in desk?"

Beth's lips tightened. She gathered up her purse and flounced out of the house.

"Thank you and goodbye," Darby murmured after the door slammed shut.

Thunder pounded overhead, making the windows shake again.

"Now there goes a woman who is not the least bit intriguing."

Darby turned to see Garrett standing in the doorway of his den. "Who? Beth?" The windows rattled again, and Darby quickly moved deeper into the living room. Away from the windows. ''She's all right. She's just—''

''On the prowl for a man.''

She picked up several crayons that had rolled from the coffee table to the floor. ''I bet you say that about all women.''

''I wouldn't say that about you.''

She pushed the crayons into the box. ''Am I supposed to be flattered by that or insulted?''

He crouched down beside her, reaching for the red crayon that she'd missed under the table. ''Neither. It's just another intriguing thing about you.''

Darby snatched the crayon out of his hand and jammed it into the box with the others. ''Stop calling me intriguing. I'm nothing of the sort.''

''Did you ever go to college?''

She stood up so fast that she felt light-headed. ''What? Yes.''

''What did you study?''

''Is this your version of Twenty Questions?'' He kept watching her, and her lips tightened. ''Nursing,'' she said shortly. ''Now, I've got to get dinner started.''

He followed her into the kitchen. ''That explains this, then.'' He held up his hand. His cut had healed enough that it was covered only with an adhesive bandage. ''So why are you playing nursery worker instead of nurse?''

''I didn't say I *was* one.'' Darby grabbed a deep pot and filled it with water. She wasn't one anymore, that's for sure. Nurses were licensed and licenses could be traced. ''We're having spaghetti. But we don't have any garlic bread. Would you mind running to the store to get some?'' Anything, anything to get him to move away. To get him out of her personal space so she could think of something more than the way he smelled so warm and male and—

"In other words you don't want to discuss your nursing aspirations."

She turned the water up higher.

"Garlic bread," he murmured. "I'll see what I can do." He smiled faintly and left.

Darby drew in a deep breath and let it out in a rush.

What a mess she'd gotten herself into.

She turned off the water and set the pot on the stove, glancing out the window at Regan and Reid who were chasing each other around in the backyard, perfectly oblivious to the crackling thunder.

A mess she was beginning to feel awfully comfortable in.

Chapter Eight

"Relax, would you?" Hayden spoke softly as he leaned a few inches toward Garrett. "I've heard Judge March is a pretty straight shooter, but if he sees you looking as if the top of your head is going to explode, he might think you're a risky choice for guardian."

Garrett forced his hands to relax. Hayden was right, he knew. "Courtrooms," he said grimly. "Haven't ever liked 'em much."

"Probably because you were on the receiving end of justice," Hayden murmured. "It was a long time ago. Forget it. You are a nation-wide developer. You can hold your own against anyone now, including the mayor."

Garrett sure as hell hoped so.

The judge, beanpole tall and white-haired, entered the courtroom and everyone present rose, sitting again only after the judge impatiently waved at them.

Garrett glanced back over the small crowd that had been gathering. Darby sat in the back row. A wide-brimmed straw hat sat on her head, preventing him from seeing her expression. He doubted that it had changed much, though, since earlier that morning when Carmel had arrived at the house. His assistant had agreed to watch the children during the hearing, and Garrett suspected that it was only Carmel's presence that had kept Darby from backing out entirely.

Since he'd brought up that nursing thing the evening before, she'd barely spoken to him.

Judge March was eyeing the courtroom. "Seems we've got a lot of spectators," he commented. "This isn't a hockey match so I'm gonna ask the sheriff here to clear the courtroom."

Voices murmured, and feet shuffled reluctantly from the courtroom. Garrett looked back again. Darby had left, too. Without her, his case was toast.

"Morning, Mayor," the judge was saying. "I'm real sorry about your daughter. I'm real sorry about us being here today at all. Seems like situations like this always get worse before they get better." He shook his head and slid a pair of eyeglasses on his beaked nose. "Let's try to keep this as uncomplicated as we can. I'd like to get out of here before lunch. Any arguments?" He eyed the occupants of both tables and with none forthcoming, nodded with satisfaction. "All right, then."

Darby felt as if a dozen curious eyes were watching her and, wanting only to escape, she walked down the wide marble-floored hallway toward the drinking fountain. She slipped her hat off long enough to bend over the bubbler and take a quick drink.

But the cool, refreshing water did little to alleviate the tension that clawed at her. Until the accident had occurred on the corner outside of Smiling Faces, she'd almost managed to forget the fear of being recognized.

Going to the market had become something to enjoy rather than something to dread. Walking in the park was no longer an exercise in furtiveness, but something to cherish. Now it was all back. In spades.

From beneath the brim of her summer hat, she eyed the crowd that was still hovering outside of the courtroom doors. At least four of them were reporters. She would have recognized the look of them even without the steno pads or the microcassette recorders.

The exit was right behind her. So close she could feel it reaching out to her. Beckoning. Inviting her to slip out the doors. To start running. To keep going, not stopping until she'd found a new place…another haven where she could start anew. Where she was still just a normal woman.

Just thinking it made her breathless. She actually pressed her hand against the heavy wooden panel. One push and she'd be through. She'd go and keep going.

She stared at her splayed fingers. Garrett had to regret what had happened between them when his father had come by the house the day he'd been working on the plumbing. Other than his unexpected appearance at the hospital, he'd been back to his usual self. He hadn't even eaten dinner with her and the children after he'd returned with the garlic bread. He'd just left the foil-covered loaf on the counter, asked her to leave out her car keys so he could arrange to have her car returned from the hospital, reminded her about the hearing and shut himself in the den.

No more spontaneous laughter. No more projects around the house. No more kisses…

Not that she wanted any, of course.

It was just as well that he'd gone back to being Mr. Business.

The only thing Garrett wanted from her was help with the children and to give her account of the accident at this hearing. He didn't understand her reluctance, and she couldn't give him the reason for it. She'd seen custody hearings up close and personal. She'd have to lift her hand and swear truthfulness. Could she do that, without telling her true name?

Could she protect herself at the expense of Elise's dying words?

She inhaled shakily and dropped her hand, turning once more to face the closed courtroom doors. Her legs felt like wet noodles, and she sat down on one of the cold stone benches bracketing the double doors leading into the courtroom. She folded her hands in her lap.

And waited.

Ballet lessons. Riding lessons. Lessons of every kind and size and shape. Followed by an Ivy League education.

Garrett returned Hayden's look. Caldwell had been waxing eloquent for so long about the childhood he'd given his precious Elise that it was enough to make Garrett gag.

Instead, he watched the judge's expression as Caldwell went on and on. Almost rambling. But if the judge had feelings one way or another about what he was hearing, there was no hint of it in his expression. Any more than there'd been an indication of what he'd thought of Garrett's qualifications to care for the children when he'd been on the stand himself.

"This claim of Garrett's that Elise wanted her children to live with him can be nothing but a fabrication, and for him to drag us through this farce of—"

Hayden objected and the judge wearily rubbed his eyes. "That's enough, Mayor. We all know your feelings on this. You've made them plain enough. Why don't you return to your seat. Mr. Southerland, if you'd call in your witness, I'd like to hear what she has to say."

Garrett didn't bat an eye when Caldwell stepped down from the witness box, his brows pulled fiercely together as he looked Garrett's way. Caldwell's animosity didn't faze him any more than it ever did.

But he waited, still, when Hayden stepped out of the courtroom for a moment. The second he was gone stretched Garrett's nerves to screaming. But there she was. Walking back into the courtroom with Hayden. Looking cool and delicate in her filmy white ankle-length dress and straw hat.

Her eyes looked his way as she passed between the two tables where the opponents sat. Her husky voice trembled as she was sworn in, and when she stepped up into the witness box and sat down, he could see she was pale.

A pulse visibly beat in her throat. She rested her arms over the wooden chair arms casually enough, but Garrett could see the white knuckles from fingers curled too tightly over the ends.

"Now, Ms. White, why don't you tell us how you came to be involved in this set-to."

"Your Honor," Hayden rose. "If you'd permit me to—"

The judge waved his hand impatiently. "Sit down, Counselor. I'm getting a headache from the lot of you. I've a good mind to ban attorneys from my courtroom. Ms. White?"

Darby turned her blue gaze toward Garrett. She gave him a look he couldn't interpret, then slowly unfastened her fingers from the chair and folded them in her lap. She cleared her throat. Then, with spare words that Garrett could only admire after Caldwell's verbosity, described her actions when the terrible collision had occurred outside of her workplace. She concluded with Elise's last words.

Caldwell immediately pushed to his feet, making his chair screech against the floor. "Obviously, Elise was *not* in a stable frame of mind. And this woman's word can't be trusted, anyway! She's involved with Garrett, for God's sake."

Caldwell's attorney practically dragged his client back down onto his chair, his words fast and low. Finally Caldwell subsided and the judge turned to Darby, waiting.

"Mrs. Northrop was quite lucid, considering," Darby answered Caldwell's first point. "She knew her husband was…gone. She knew she wasn't going to make it to the hospital. She'd been carrying Mr. Cullum's business card in her purse. It was right where she said it would be."

"Did she speak of anyone else other than Mr. Cullum?"

Garrett saw the telltale glisten in her eyes as she looked at Caldwell. "No," she admitted quietly. "I'm sorry."

"Any other people around who heard what she said?"

Darby shook her head. "The EMTs hadn't yet arrived." She swallowed, staring at her hands. "I kept administering CPR until they took over, but it was too late."

"Then it's just her word that Garrett didn't make this up," Caldwell burst out again. "They're in this together! All to keep me from my own flesh and blood—"

"Enough, Mayor." The judge's command rang out. "I said we were keeping this informal, because I happen to like things that way. But one more outburst and I'll hold you in contempt. Understand?"

"I...hadn't met Mr. Cullum before the accident," Darby said shakily. "But I know the children because of Smiling Faces. Garrett...Mr. Cullum, needed someone to help care for them, and I agreed."

"Which is just what the report from Laura Malone said," the judge commented. "How do you think the children are doing?"

Her lips parted, her surprise at the question evident to Garrett even if it wasn't obvious to everyone else. "Quite well," she said after a moment. "Considering. Their appetites are healthy, their sleep habits seem relatively normal. They're active, curious children. Tad does have an ear infection right now, but he's on medication for it and is improving."

"Ear infections. My grandson is plagued with them." The judge smiled slightly. "Thank you, Ms. White. You're excused."

Relief that the ordeal was over flooded through Darby. It was all she could do not to leap from the witness box. She rose and walked to the rear of the courtroom.

She didn't know if she was expected to leave or

not. But she didn't want to go out into the corridor and face the curiosity of the reporters, if they were still hanging around. And her experience of reporters led her to believe that they would be.

So she quietly slipped into a seat in the back row.

"This is a difficult situation," Judge March was saying. "Elise and Marc left no will, no provisions financial or otherwise for their children. The Northrops were, in fact, experiencing some financial difficulty as I understand it. But, as I said when we sat down here this morning, the welfare of the children is the only concern of this court."

Ten minutes later it was over. Just like that. Garrett got to keep the children.

For a while, at least.

Caldwell stormed out of the courtroom, his attorney trotting unhappily after him. When the doors swished open, she heard the rapid-fire questions begin. In a smooth motion, the door whooshed closed, blotting out the voices.

She stood and waited while Garrett spoke with his attorney. Then the other man turned to Darby and shook her hand. "You did very well on the stand."

She shifted nervously, feeling like a complete fraud, even though she had been strictly truthful about her account of the accident.

He smiled. "Not everyone does," he assured her. Then his eyes narrowed for a moment. "I keep thinking we've met."

Darby's face felt stiff. She raised her eyebrows, lifting her shoulder casually. "Don't think so." It was all she could do to push out the words.

"Well. Anyway. Thanks. Garrett, I'll see you tomorrow. We've got that meeting with Zoning tomorrow.''

''Make sure Carmel's got it on my schedule.''

Hayden nodded, then he left. Leaving Darby alone with Garrett.

She looked anywhere but at him. ''Mr. Carson is pretty upset.''

''So it seems.'' He paused for a moment. ''I wasn't sure you'd hang around after the judge kicked everyone out of the place,'' he finally said. ''I'm glad I was wrong.''

''Courtrooms,'' she excused weakly. ''Not my favorite place.''

''Nor mine. Spent too much time in 'em when I was the reigning delinquent of Fisher Falls.''

''You?'' Her gaze drifted over him. In a charcoal-colored suit fitted across his wide shoulders, his lean face once again clean shaven, his springy black hair brushed back from his face, he looked the very picture of uprightness and responsibility.

''I had a liking for hotwiring cars,'' he admitted.

Her jaw loosened. ''You stole cars?''

''I…liberated them from a certain owner with frequent regularity.''

''Mr. Carson's cars?''

His grin was slow and utterly wicked. ''Pretty and smart,'' he said. ''Come on. Let's get outta here.''

She kept her smile in place with an effort. *Please, let the reporters be gone.* ''Carmel is probably tearing her hair out by now.''

''She'd be saying that no matter how well things went. Figures it'll keep me feeling guilty. But I'm not ready to go home. I thought we'd go somewhere for lunch. You know. Somewhere that doesn't involve finger foods and sipper cups. You game?''

She moistened her lips. ''I'm not sure that's a good idea.''

''We need to talk about the kids.''

''We don't have to go to a restaurant to do that.''

''Humor me.''

It was a mistake. She knew it. But looking at him, all she could think about at that moment was the way he'd tipped back his head into the mud the other day and laughed. ''Garrett—''

He nudged back the brim of her hat. ''The Overlook,'' he murmured. ''They have a dessert menu there that'll make you cry. And if not that, at least lick your lips.''

She felt her ears heat, realizing she had pretty well done just that as she'd watched his mouth form his words. ''I don't know. I hear it's a pricey place.''

''I think I can swing it,'' he said dryly.

She pressed her lips together, looking away. ''I...all right. But we really shouldn't be out long. It wouldn't be fair to Carmel.''

He nodded once, satisfied, and pushed open the door for her to pass through. She was so distracted by the hand he tucked against the small of her back that she barely remembered to adjust her hat as she walked out into the corridor.

But she needn't have worried, because the wide hallway was empty. The spectators, reporters included, had gone and for a moment she felt weak with relief.

Garrett jabbed the elevator button and looked at her. ''You all right? You look a little shaky.''

She managed a smile. ''I must be hungrier than I thought. Didn't smell my coffee this morning.''

He didn't look convinced, but the elevator doors slid open and Darby stepped into the nearly full car before he could comment. Lunch hour was obviously calling to the government workers who populated the top floors of the pillared building.

The occupants shifted, making room for Garrett's tall body, and Darby found herself wedged into the corner. She swallowed and looked up at the lit display above the door.

They had only three floors to descend, but it might as well have been twelve for the way the elevator seemed to grind along. She could feel her chest tightening, her lungs struggling for breath. Knowing what was happening didn't help her to prevent it. A screaming knot rose in her throat, welling, swelling upward—

The doors slid open, passengers erupting around her into the lobby.

"Come on." Garrett's arm closed around her shoulders. "Outside."

Suddenly she was outside. Fresh air filled her lungs. She felt sunlight on her arms, heard laughter from a passing group of office workers heading down the steps to the street.

She was pressed against Garrett's side, her nose buried in his shoulder. "Oh, God." She pushed away, as far as his arms allowed. Embarrassment burned inside her. "I'm sorry."

"Don't be sorry. Let's just get to the truck." He guided her down the shallow steps. "Or maybe you'd rather walk. The Overlook isn't that far from here."

"Really? You wouldn't mind walking?"

In answer, he shrugged off his suit jacket and slung it over his shoulder. "I've been known to put one foot in front of the other now and then." He smiled faintly and took her arm, walking leisurely along the tree-lined sidewalk. "But don't tell Carmel, or she'll start refusing to fetch and carry for me."

"I can't imagine there is anything that Carmel would refuse you."

"You haven't seen our Monday-morning battles over who's supposed to make the coffee."

Darby managed a smile. He was deliberately trying to put her at ease. It was so utterly backward, and he didn't even know it.

They walked on in silence. In and out of the shadows of the lacy leaves overhead. They crossed streets, left behind the business of the courthouse district, walking along a winding street that led gently upward. Past the park at the base of the waterfalls, past long, private drives that led to gracious older estates.

Estates like her aunt's.

Like Caldwell Carson's.

The road narrowed and Garrett moved to Darby's left side, between her and the sporadic traffic. On the other side of her, a waist-high stone wall guarded the edge of the increasingly deep drop-off. Below, Fisher Falls lay like a sparkling jewel. Several yards ahead, she could see the discreet sign of The Overlook.

She ran her hand along the aging stone. "It is so beautiful here."

"You make that sound like a bad thing."

"Not bad," she demurred. "Just hard to leave."

"You're planning on going somewhere?"

"Not if I can avoid it," she admitted truthfully. "Didn't you miss it when you left?" She lifted her hand, gesturing to the lush green beauty that surrounded them. "You must have. You came back."

"I came back because Fisher Falls is on the verge

of a construction boom. Business, Darby. That's all it was.''

"Now you sound like my brother again.''

"What does he do?''

She shook her head slightly. "How do you know we're on the verge of anything, much less a construction boom?''

"Trade secret.''

"In other words, you're not going to tell me.''

"You tell me something about your brother, instead of avoiding it, and I'll tell you about G&G.''

Darby stopped, pointing at the restaurant sign. "Well look at that. We're here.''

Garrett wrapped his palm around her slender finger, feeling the little jerk she couldn't hide. Darby no longer looked like she was going to pass out, but she was far from relaxed, despite the effort she'd been making to convince him otherwise. "You're shivering.''

She looked up, above their heads. "We're standing in the shade.''

"Don't do that, Darby.''

She slid her hand out from his, her fingertips fluttering nervously to her throat. "I was just a little unnerved in the elevator. That's all.'' She tried to step around him toward the rustic-looking restaurant, but Garrett shifted, blocking the path.

"*Unnerved.* Seems a puny word to me. You got claustrophobic. You don't have to hide it.''

"I'm not. I just…just— There were so many people inside the elevator. I…I was fine when we arrived, you know.''

He wouldn't go quite that far, but it was true enough. She hadn't been ready to climb out of her skin. "There were only a few people on the elevator when we took it up to the courtroom," he allowed. "So it's just overcrowded small places that get to you?"

Her cheeks were red, her eyes embarrassed. Evasive. "Something like that."

Embarrassment he could understand, even though it wasn't necessary. The evasiveness was another matter.

"Does it have anything to do with this?" He rubbed his thumb gently over her throat, and he felt her nervous swallow. "The injury to your vocal chords?"

"Why does it matter?"

"It still affects you."

"So?"

He kept his patience with an effort. "So I'm interested in—"

Her eyes widened.

"—in your...welfare," he finished, taking his hand from her smooth neck and pushing it into his pocket. Everyone was entitled to their privacy, he reminded himself. Wondering when the hell he'd forgotten it. "You've helped me out. I owe you."

"No." She shook her head, her expression growing even more pained. "You don't owe me anything, Garrett. You really don't."

She might as well have posted Keep Away banners around herself. Unfortunately, Garrett couldn't remember why he should be glad of that.

He looked at her mouth. What he did remember was the way she'd tasted. Of sunshine and cold water from the hose. Of smiles and laughter from kids who were hardly even old enough to know they had little reason to laugh.

"Well, I hope that doesn't mean you've decided

against lunch.'' He lifted his chin toward the restaurant. ''Now that you've made me hoof it all this way.''

''*Made* you—'' Her mouth snapped shut. ''You're teasing me again,'' she finally said.

''Maybe.''

She sighed noisily. But he could still see the twitch at the corner of her soft lips. ''Why?'' she asked tartly. ''Why do you do that?''

He shrugged and nudged her toward the restaurant. ''Because I'm beginning to think you have had as few smiles in your life as I've had in mine.''

Chapter Nine

Darby shook her head when the waiter offered her coffee and watched him fill Garrett's ivory cup. "I don't know how you can just sit there so relaxed when Mayor Carson is right across this very dining room glaring at us."

"His presence is bugging you a hell of a lot more 'n it's bugging me."

"Obviously."

The corner of Garrett's mobile mouth twitched. "But it does show that this town ain't big enough for the two of us," he added.

She twisted the linen napkin in her lap another knot or two. The small table she and Garrett shared was next to the window, and she shifted the last available inch to look outside. The mayor had come into the restaurant after Darby and Garrett had already been served. "I've always hated being watched." She shifted again, uncomfortable.

"Then you should walk around with a bag over your head," he suggested.

Pleasure darted guiltily through her. Three months ago she'd hacked off her waist-length hair with sewing shears and begun dressing in the most bland clothing imaginable. She'd wanted nothing to connect her to the woman she'd been. The woman who wore only vibrant, couturier clothing because her father expected it was no more.

"You said you wanted to talk about the kids," she reminded them both. "That was the whole point of this lunch. Wasn't it?"

"Which you ate very little of," Garrett pointed out.

"It was enormous." She'd dutifully poked and prodded at the elaborate mound of chicken and lettuce and fifty other ingredients because Garrett expected her to, not because she'd had any real appetite. The day's activities had taken care of that. "The children...?"

Garrett's large hand eclipsed the delicate china coffee cup as he lowered it to the saucer. "You heard the judge," he said as he signed the credit slip and pocketed his gold credit card. "He's not happy at all that I'm single. That I show none of the makings of a 'family' man.

"My only edge over Caldwell is that I'm not old enough to be their grandfather. I've only been awarded temporary custody. Six weeks to prove—or disprove, as Caldwell over there obviously hopes—my suitability as a guardian."

"I don't think that's necessarily a bad thing."

His lips twisted. "So you think I'm a bad bet, too."

"I didn't say that. Garrett, honestly, I don't think that at all." Stunned, she sat forward, pressing her hand over his. "Do you?"

He was looking at her hand on his. Which made her look at her hand on his. Swallowing, she sat back in her chair, pressing both her hands against the twisted cloth in her lap. "Do you?" she asked again.

"I didn't plan to be in Fisher Falls that long," he said instead of answering.

"Oh." She wasn't sure where the flood of disappointment came from, but she knew she didn't like it. "I didn't realize. I, um, I thought you'd moved here. You know, permanently. To run that construction company."

"I own that construction company. And I'm only here to get things up and running. Once that's underway, I'm gone, leaving one extremely competent team behind."

"Own?" She blinked. "Well. Don't I feel the fool."

"Why?"

"Ah…because. I didn't know."

"We could feast on all the information we don't know about each other." He stood. "I asked the hostess to call us a taxi. I imagine it's here by now. You ready?"

Her stomach clutched a little. She dropped her napkin on the table and rose. He took her elbow, and she started.

"I thought you'd relaxed over the lunch you didn't eat." He guided her through the dining room toward the entrance.

It was only because she was no longer accustomed to a man escorting her around, she told herself. Not because it was Garrett's hand on her arm. "I did relax. And I did eat. I just didn't eat as much as you."

His lips tilted, amused. But the faint grin died when Caldwell appeared in the doorway.

The older man's angry eyes took in them both. "I won't let you steal my grandchildren from me."

"You're showing a decided lack of sportsmanship, Caldwell."

Darby caught her breath. "Garrett—"

"And you." Caldwell turned his attention to Darby, and the cautionary words died in her throat at the torment in the mayor's eyes. "How much is he paying you to keep up this story of yours?" he demanded. "I'll triple it."

She stiffened. His offer stung like a harsh slap. "My integrity is not for sale, Mayor Carson."

"Is anything else about you for sale?"

She stared at him. "I beg your pardon?"

Garrett's expression frosted over and he stepped close to his father, topping him by only an inch in height. "You might want to apologize while you can, Mayor."

"I have no intention of apologizing. What you two are doing is criminal. Amoral. Taking advantage of Elise's death. Cavorting in front of innocent children, then abandoning them to God only knows who while you play footsie—"

"Watch it, old man. That's your future daughter-in-law you're insulting."

Darby blinked, staring at Garrett. "What are you—"

Garrett's arm slid around her shoulder, and she found herself pulled snugly and securely against his warm side. The words died in her throat.

Caldwell was staring at them both. "You're getting married?"

"As soon as it can be arranged."

She couldn't believe what she was hearing. "Garrett, I—"

"It's all right, darlin'. There's no point in keeping it a secret. Caldwell *is* family, after all."

"You didn't say anything about this in court today. This is just another part of your plot to keep my grandchildren from me."

Beside her Garrett shrugged, and her temper finally flared. "I'm appalled at both of you! You," she poked Garrett in the chest with a furious finger, "are acting as if this is some great big game, just as I expected all along. And you," she turned to point at the mayor, "are just as bad. The only family those poor children have left are the two of you, and look at the way you are behaving! Maybe the judge shouldn't choose *either* of you."

The flash of anger drained away, leaving an aching heaviness in its wake. If it weren't for her, these two men wouldn't be using the children as the rope in their personal tug of war. "And I shouldn't be involved at all," she finished. She turned on her heel and ran over to the waiting taxi, slipping into the back seat before anyone could stop her.

Garrett watched the cab drive away. "That was low, Caldwell. Even for you."

"What is low, Garrett, is what you're doing. If you want to take me on businesswise, you go right ahead. Castle Construction is more than a match for G&G, and you know as well as I do that this town isn't large enough to support two major firms. But I won't let you steal away my grandchildren like this."

"The court decided it. So I suggest you learn to live with it." He started down the sidewalk. Darby had used the taxi, so he'd just walk back to his truck, still parked near the courthouse. "As for Fisher Falls being large enough for only one of us?" His lips stretched in a cold smile. "I'm counting on it."

He turned and strode down the driveway, the pleasure that he'd felt on the walk to The Overlook gone. And that lack had nothing to do with Caldwell's pain-in-the-ass comments. It had everything to do with Darby's absence, and the look in her sky-blue eyes when she'd run away.

Disappointment.

By the time he'd retrieved his truck and driven back to his rental, he'd convinced himself that Darby would be packed and gone from the house. So the sight of the pathetic green monstrosity she drove still parked at the curb was a distinct relief. It was right where he'd had it returned late last night.

He strode inside, stopping short at the sight of Carmel standing in the living room. She was all but wringing her hands together. "Thank goodness you're finally back."

"What's wrong? Where are the kids?"

Carmel looked toward the staircase. "Wonder of wonders, they're all taking naps. They're fine. It's Darby. She's gone."

"*Gone?* What do you mean *gone?* Her car's parked outside."

"It wouldn't start."

"How long ago? I was only a half hour behind her, at the most." He took the stairs two at a time, bursting into the master bedroom.

The bed was neatly made, Darby's wide-brimmed

straw hat sitting on the foot of it. The cribs lined up like stalwart soldiers against the wall, guarding the sleeping tots who lay inside.

He went into the attached bathroom. She'd left behind a bar of soap, sitting in the soap holder on the edge of the sink. He touched the smooth, dry cake, but that one touch was enough to leave the tip of his finger smelling like vanilla.

Like Darby.

He turned to see Carmel watching him, her eyebrows raised. He shoved his hand in his pocket and went out into the hall, softly closing the bedroom door behind him. "How long ago?" he asked again. "Did she say where she was going?"

"About twenty minutes ago. And I'd assume, home."

He muttered an oath. "Did she say anything else?"

"Other than that you and Caldwell are two of a kind?" Carmel shook her head. "Not much."

"Two of a kind. God." The idea was repugnant, but not one he hadn't thought more than once himself. "Listen, Carmel. I need you to do me a favor."

"No. No way. Uh-uh. I've got work at the office. Remember the office? G&G? The reason why we're holed up here in this town that's right out of a Norman Rockwell?"

"It shouldn't take me more 'n an hour." He looked at his watch, calculating. "Better make it two. Or three."

"I'm not staying here with those children while you go chasing after Darby." She followed furiously on his heels when he headed back down the stairs. "She's not the only person in town who can watch them!"

"I don't want anyone else."

"But—"

"Carmel, please. Call Hayden. He'll come and help you."

Her expression tightened. "I don't need your attorney's help."

"Then don't call him." Garrett didn't care. "Three hours." He left the house on Carmel's muttered Spanish. She was cursing his ancestors, his future progeny and all points in between.

He started up his truck and drove back toward the center of town. He caught up to Darby on Riverside. The same road they'd walked earlier on the way to The Overlook.

Her soft-sided overnight bag, its long strap slung over one shoulder, bumped against her hip with each step she took. He slowed his truck, pulling up beside her.

The look she gave him should have singed the hair off his body. She angled her head, adjusting the wide strap on her shoulder, and trudged on, ignoring him. He sighed and took his foot off the gas, the powerful engine creeping along.

"You've got a long way to walk before you get to Georgie's place."

"One foot in front of the other."

Her voice was as cool and imperious as a princess. Totally at odds with her screwball haircut and mutinous chin. "We never did get a chance to talk about the kids."

She shot him an incredulous look. Her mouth parted, as if she was searching for words. But none came. Her lips tightened and she faced forward again, her steps quickening.

"I know you're angry with me, but I didn't think you'd take it out on the kids."

She stopped. His foot hit the brake.

"Don't do that," she said tightly. "Don't use the kids to manipulate me into doing what you want. It's...it's...unworthy of you."

Unworthy. Which just went to show how little she really knew about him. "I'm sorry." And he almost was. Only because he hated, really hated, the look of disappointment that was still clouding her pretty blue eyes. He pulled up to the curb and shut off the engine, climbing out.

She backed up warily, not stopping until she bumped the waist-high stone wall behind her.

He lifted his hands peaceably. "Come on home, Darby."

"Home?" Her eyebrows skyrocketed. "I don't have a home. Certainly not one with you. *How* could you tell your father that you and I are getting married? How could you lie like that?"

"It wasn't a lie." He moved across the sidewalk. "It's the perfect answer, Darby. You love the kids."

"I don't—"

"Of course you do." He swallowed his impatience, knowing that it was definitely not the time or place for that particular flaw of his. "It's obvious. And they love you. You've already admitted that you're not involved with anyone else."

"Oh, so *obviously* I must be available for something as insignificant as *marriage?*" She shook her head. "I cannot believe you."

"Don't put words in my mouth."

"Don't go around telling people that I'm going to

be your wife!'' Her voice rose with each word. She colored and pressed her hand over her eyes.

Her shaking hand, he noticed.

''Let's go somewhere where we can discuss this,'' he suggested quietly.

Her hand dropped. ''There is nothing to discuss.''

''Then give me a chance to explain, at least.''

''I can't marry you.''

''Can't? Not won't?''

Her lips twisted. ''Won't then. The very idea is ridiculous.''

''Why?''

''Why? *Why?*'' Her hands lifted. Pushed through her red-blond-brown hair. ''We've known each other for only ten days! The other proposals I've received at least came from men I'd known more than two weeks.''

''Proposals with an *s*. How many does that mean?''

''Three. But only one did I take seriously, and for all his faults he at least had the decency to ask me before announcing it to all and sundry.''

''I thought you said there was no one.''

''There isn't.'' She turned away from him, staring out over the fence, out over the rocky drop-off to the jewel-green valley below. ''There hasn't been for two years.''

''He's the one you're running from, then.''

Her spine stiffened as if rebar had just replaced it. ''Why on earth would you say something like that?''

''You're not denying it.''

Her jaw worked. ''Of course I'm denying it.''

''What brought you to Fisher Falls, Darby?''

''Georgina Vansant,'' she answered tightly. ''Are

these the standard questions on the job application for a prospective Mrs. Garrett Cullum?''

''And the joker who proposed to you had nothing to do with it?''

''The *joker* was my fiancé. Until he decided he preferred his ex-wife, the mother of his children, over me.''

It was so far from what he'd begun to suspect that Garrett couldn't think *what* to say.

Her eyes glistened, her expression pained. ''What? No smart answers? No quick retort? No smooth thinking to turn that to your advantage?''

He wasn't used to tenderness. Feeling it. Expressing it. That wasn't what his life had been about. But the sight of the silvery tear slipping down her smooth cheek nearly undid him. He wanted to wrap her in cotton. Protect her from any more pain. ''What—'' he had to clear his throat ''—what happened?''

''That's none of your business.'' She stepped around him, heading once more along the road. ''It's none of anyone's business.''

Garrett slammed his palms against the wall. The rough, aged stone scraped him. Cut. It was nothing compared to watching Darby walk away from him. Again.

Had he ever made such a mess of anything in his life?

Everything he said was wrong.

Everything he did was wrong.

He'd started out just wanting a caring nanny for his sister's kids so his conscience would let him sleep at night.

When had he managed to so completely screw it all up?

He crossed the sidewalk, reaching for the truck door just as Darby crossed the street to head up the mile-long private road of the Vansant estate.

As she did, a white van came barreling along the road, screeching to a halt as it passed Darby. A man jumped out the passenger side door and approached Darby.

Garrett saw her shake her head, try to walk around the man. That's all he waited to see. He jumped behind the wheel, gunning the engine, heading for the private drive. His truck easily bumped over the curb, and he cut in front of the television station van.

He saw the flash of Darby's pale, startled expression. The frustration on the face of the news anchorman's. "Get in," he told Darby harshly.

"I just want a comment for tonight's segment," the newsman shouted after them. "We're running a report of the accident investigation!"

Apparently, Garrett's company was less objectionable than the newsman's, because Darby ran in front of his truck and scrambled up into the passenger seat. He drove around the van, heading up the drive toward the estate.

"Go to the gatehouse."

He looked over at Darby. Her husky voice had been barely audible.

"Where?"

She pointed. He took the right fork in the road, heading away from the grand main house, moving at a fast clip between the high hedges and the vibrant rows of summer flowers.

There, at the end of the road, was a small building. The gatehouse. He parked in front of the door, rounded the truck and opened Darby's side.

She was trembling. Staring at her hands.

"I hate reporters." Her voice shook. "Vultures. All of them. Why can't they let people be? Why does everything have to be a damn story?"

He started to reach for her but didn't. "Darby."

She didn't look at him. Her hands still rested in her lap. Pale, pale hands. Palms up against the white fabric of her floaty dress.

"I'm out of my element here," he admitted. Claustrophobic in a crowded elevator. An ex-fiancé she was not running from. An absolute aversion to reporters. "Tell me how to help you."

Her long, elegant fingers curled into small fists. "I don't need your help. I don't need your marriage proposal. Such as it was." She shifted, sliding out of the truck and walking past him toward the gatehouse. "I don't need anyone."

Chapter Ten

Marry him.

The idea was insane.

Darby's hand shook so badly she could barely fit the door key into the lock. When she finally succeeded, she practically threw herself into the haven that Georgie had allowed her when she'd arrived in Fisher Falls.

She didn't know why she didn't close and lock the door after her.

To do so would surely have kept Garrett out. Which was only the sensible thing to do.

She dumped her overnight bag on the tile floor and moved across the square room to the other side, where windows overlooked the edge of the Vansant property.

Wild, wooded.

It was the sight that she'd wakened to for the three months that she'd lived in the gatehouse. Only from the rear of the main house was the view different. The windows there overlooked the beautiful waterfall that gave the town its name.

She had never had someone inside the gatehouse. Not even Georgie visited her down here.

Now *he* was here.

Walking through the door and closing it behind him as if she'd invited him. As if he had every right, every reason to be there.

Darby turned around, pressing her palms flat against the cool windowpane behind her.

"Everyone needs someone," he said. His intent gaze drifted over the cozy interior of the gatehouse. Noting everything, she felt sure. From the blue-and-yellow chintz sofa to the mini-kitchen against one wall with the pale-yellow sink and tiny refrigerator.

"Not everyone." Her father, for one. Dane for another. "If you had just let the mayor take your nieces and nephews, you wouldn't need anyone, either." Dammit, she hadn't meant to bring that up. She'd meant only to get him out of there. Out of her only haven.

That she would now forever remember him invading.

She realized he was looking at the shelves surrounding the small television in the corner and deliberately moved into his line of vision, drawing his gaze away from the small collection of photos she'd placed there. "Why, Garrett? Why me? You don't even know me. Why tell your...tell the mayor such an outrageous lie?"

"I told you. It doesn't have to be a lie."

Her hands pressed to her stomach, but nothing could

take away the ache she felt deep inside. "It cannot be the truth."

"There are five good reasons for it to be the truth," he said. "Regan, Reid, Tad, Bridget and Keely." He nudged her down onto the sofa, sitting beside her. The fluffy, flouncy, feminine fabric made him look even darker. More dangerous. "Listen. It's the perfect answer. Consider it a job, if it makes you feel better."

"A job," she echoed.

"A few years as my wife. At least until Regan and Reid are both in elementary school. You'll be well compensated."

"Well, golly. I guess I should just leap right at that delightful offer." She jumped to her feet, moving away from him. Far away, where she could think clearly again. "Between you and your father, one would think I'd do anything in exchange for the almighty dollar."

"I'm not trying to insult you."

She smiled humorlessly. "I'd hate to see how well you could accomplish it if you *did* try."

He leaned forward, resting his arms on his thighs. Somewhere along the way he'd gotten rid of his suit coat and rolled up his shirtsleeves. He linked his fingers together, looking as casual and easy as if they were discussing the color of rice.

Since she figured she had as little hope of rousting him from the gatehouse as she did of turning back time, she focused on the way the afternoon sunlight glinted on his gold wristwatch.

"Darby, all I'm trying to do—badly, I admit—is be fair. I don't expect you to go along with us and get nothing in return."

"Well. It's a change of pace, I admit," she said

wearily. Bryan hadn't wanted to marry her, after all, no matter how much money her father threw his way. Now Garrett was offering to pay *her* to gain a more permanent caretaker for his nieces and nephews.

At least for a few years, according to him.

"Why marriage?" she asked. "You started out wanting a nanny. What happened to that?"

"You heard Caldwell. He's not going to stop this…campaign of his until he wins."

"Wins!" She turned on her heel, crossing to the kitchenette. "There you go again. Acting as if it is some contest to be won. Are either one of you thinking about what the children need? What the children want?"

"That's why I need you. Because you *do* think of the children. First. Not as an afterthought, or as an obligation. But because you actually do care for them."

She shook her head. "No. I can't do it. I agreed to…watch them for this week. Remember that agreement?" It seemed like ages ago, but it truthfully had been only one week. "Find somebody else."

"Where am I going to find anyone who cares as much for them as you do?"

She raised her arms, turning around to glare at him. "Hire someone off the street. It's practically what you've tried to do with me!"

He just looked at her.

And she wanted to turn around and run. Run away. Just as she'd done three months ago.

Only running had led her to Fisher Falls and that, in turn, had led Phil Candela there. To that corner outside of Smiling Faces at the same moment as Elise and Marc Northrop. Running had caused this situation.

And already her arms felt empty from being away from the children.

Oh, God. It was that kind of thinking that had gotten her involved with Garrett and his "fearsome five" in the first place.

"No," she shook her head. "No. No way."

He rose from the couch, walking toward her. "What are you afraid of?"

She backed up. Bumped the yellow tiled counter behind her. "Nothing."

"Tad, Bridget and Keely are so young they'll think of you as their mother. Reid, too, most likely."

His green eyes saw too much. She held his gaze with an effort. "But I'm not their mother," she said carefully. "I never will be. They're your nieces and nephews, and even if I did agree to this ridiculous idea that you've come up with, that wouldn't change. Somewhere down the line, whether it's when Regan and Reid are finally in school or not, you'd decide you didn't need me anymore, or...or you'd want to marry someone else for real." Her throat was tight, the words emerging with difficulty. "And I'd be lost."

His eyes gentled. "You won't be lost, Darby."

"You don't know."

"I know what I can promise. There isn't going to be someone to come along that I want to marry 'for real.' I never planned to marry at all. Until now."

"Garrett, please. A man like you—"

He waited.

And she was suddenly, painfully aware of the silence surrounding them. "Well. I mean, there must be women in your life or who will come into your life. You'll date and...get involved."

"I'm already involved," he murmured.

"There you go, then." She forced a smile. "Get her to marry you."

"I'm trying to."

That silence, that intimate, seductive silence twined around them again. "You and I—" She swallowed. "We're not involved."

"Feels like we're getting there to me."

She moistened her lips. "If that were true, which it *isn't*, you're already setting things up to fail. Planning a marriage that will last only a few years. That's no way to live. Believe me. I know."

He touched her shoulder, his hand warm and hard and indefinably gentle. "How do you know?"

She hunched, trying to move out from that tempting touch. She didn't succeed. And the loose strap slipped off her shoulder, stopped only by Garrett's long fingers. "I just do," she said irritably.

His head tilted, the corner of his lips deepening. "Something wrong?" he asked mildly.

She stalled her motion to adjust her dress strap. "I don't like being crowded."

"Ah, Darby. How many words that come out of your mouth are actually true?"

She flinched. "Then you surely wouldn't want such a compulsive liar to be your convenient wife."

"Darby?"

"What?"

"Shut up."

Her lips parted. His head lowered, his mouth fitting over hers. She caught her breath. Breathing him. Inhaling him. His scent. His taste. He was intoxicating.

She frowned, grappling for sense, twisting her lips from his. "Garrett—"

His kiss ran along her jaw, touched her ear.

She moaned and angled her head away again. He merely transferred his attention to her shoulder. The shoulder that was bare of the dress strap. "This isn't, ah, sensible."

"I find it remarkably sensible." He slid his palm against the small of her back, lifted her hand and pressed his mouth to the tender skin in the crook of her elbow.

Her fingers curled. Her knees sagged. He kissed her jaw again. Driving her mad. "I don't do this sort of thing," she protested desperately. And shocked herself right down to her core when she thrust her fingers through his hair and drew his mouth back to hers.

His arms tightened around her, pulling her close. Ever closer. She couldn't seem to remember why this was wrong. Not when he felt so good. Not when his hands, so sure, so wonderfully male, so perfectly him, slid over her hips, lifting her.

She gasped, but he was setting her on the tiled counter, stepping between her knees, his touch burning through her dress. No, not through her dress. On her skin. Her knees. Her thighs. Her—

"No." Darby pressed her hands against his chest. His bare chest. Had she done that? Had she unbuttoned his shirt like that? Pulled it free of his trousers? She yanked her hands back, folding them together, determined to keep them under control. "We can't. I can't. I'm your...nanny."

"Fiancée," he countered. "And not just for convenience. We'd have a real marriage. It wouldn't be a name-only thing."

He ran his fingertip along the neckline of her dress, and she wondered if her heart would just burst right out of her chest it beat so hard.

"We could try it," he continued, "if it makes you feel better. But I'm telling you right now, it wouldn't work."

"No." She caught his wandering finger.

A muscle ticked unevenly in his jaw. "No?"

He very deliberately stepped back from her, holding his hands slightly out from his sides.

She covered her eyes for a moment, shaking. "You don't know who I am."

"I know enough."

"No, Garrett." She looked into his eyes. Feeling herself becoming absorbed by that deep, dark green. "You don't. I'm—"

"I know this." With one smooth swoop, he took her lips with his.

Her head reeled. He touched her nowhere else. Just his mouth on hers. His lips rubbing ever so gently across hers. Then he straightened. She swayed, feeling bereft.

"The first time I saw you," he said roughly. "I knew that. But I figured it was smarter to ignore it."

"And now?"

"I can't ignore it anymore." His gaze felt like a caress on her skin. "Can you?"

She slid off the counter, yanking her dress strap into place. She walked across the room. Back to the windows and that wild, wooded view. But sudden tears obscured it, and she closed her eyes, pressing her fists against her temples.

"Bryan had two children. *Has* two children." She swallowed. How easily she saw them in her mind. "Bobby was six, then. Amy was four. Bryan had custody, you see. We were going to be a family. The three of us. I was finally going to have the kind of life I'd dreamed of. A family who was together. Who stayed together. Forever."

She felt Garrett behind her. His hands closed gently over her shoulders, and she just wasn't strong enough to resist. She leaned back against him, sighing. Beneath her cheek she felt the hard contours of his bare chest and knew she should move away. She just couldn't quite make herself do it.

"What happened?"

"I was wrong. He changed his mind. I lost them all. And now you're suggesting I walk into the same situation."

His thumbs smoothed over her skin. "It's not the same."

"Close enough," she whispered. There *were* a lot of differences between the two situations. But the bottom line was one and the same. "I couldn't bear to walk away from your 'fearsome five.' And sooner or later, I'd have to."

"What if I guarantee that won't happen?" His words whispered over her forehead.

"Oh, Garrett. There are no guarantees. You of all people should realize that."

"What I know is that every time I follow my gut, I land on my feet. It got me from being a fifteen-year-old delinquent to where I am today. And my gut is telling me this is the right thing. I knew it the second I said it."

Her lips twisted. "I remember my anatomy classes. That's not your gut talking."

His hands turned her around until she was facing him. "Yeah. It is. Even if I wasn't battling the urge to lock ourselves into a bedroom for about a month of

Sundays, I'd still think this was the answer for us both."

"I'm not looking for any answers."

"That's because you're afraid. Of being hurt again."

She opened her mouth to deny it. But what was the point? She *didn't* want to be hurt again. She didn't want to love someone else's children, envision a life together, plan for it, only to have it all yanked away. "You're not afraid of ever being hurt?"

"It takes a heart to be hurt, Darby."

She looked at him. This man who was fighting tooth and nail to make sure he followed through on his sister's last wish. "You...don't think you have a heart," she realized sadly. "Why would you think that?"

"Whether I like admitting it or not, I am Caldwell's son."

"And he's heartless, therefore you must be, too," she concluded softly.

He was wrong. About himself. And, she suspected, about Caldwell, too. A heartless person couldn't fake the pain she'd seen in the mayor's eyes. But she knew Garrett didn't want to hear that from her.

"The children need you, Darby."

"What about you?" She couldn't believe the words came out of her mouth. But there they were. Hovering in the air between them, large as life.

His green gaze drifted to her lips. "I think we've established how I feel about you. One way or another you're gonna end up in my bed. I might as well keep it good and proper."

She didn't know how she could feel such sadness for someone and still want to bean him on the head. "Killing two birds with one stone, as it were. Satisfying your—'' her cheeks heated ''—urge and the judge all in one.''

''It's more than an urge,'' he said, amused. ''And I don't think you'd be terribly disappointed, either.''

''Pretty confident, aren't you?''

''You want me to lie and tell you I think we'll be awful together?'' He flicked the tail of his shirt. The shirt *she'd* yanked from his trousers. The shirt *she'd* unwittingly unbuttoned.

She flushed hotly.

He moved away from her, glancing around. ''I need a piece of paper.''

She frowned, started to reach for a drawer where she kept a small collection of note cards. But he'd already pulled a paper napkin from the holder on the counter by the sink. He sat down on the sofa, scrawling rapidly on the napkin, using the silly sparkly pink pen she'd brought home from one of the birthday parties at Smiling Faces. Then he held the napkin out to her.

She automatically took it. ''What is this?''

''Terms.''

She read. And had to sit down, herself. ''A prenup.''

''More or less.''

She looked at the sparkly pink scrawl again. It was brief and to the point. Only he didn't specify that, in the event of the demise of their marriage, what was his would remain his and vice versa.

What he did specify was that she would retain joint custody of the children. And lifetime support.

For a moment she thought she might be ill.

''It's only fair,'' he said evenly. ''You're the only reason I've got a chance at fulfilling Elise's wish.

You're the one who cares most about them. Sometimes I even get the feeling that you're the one who is hurting the most over the accident.'' He reached out and brushed his thumb over her cheek. ''You're the only one who has cried for them.''

She carefully set the napkin on the coffee table. ''You said you'd remain in Fisher Falls until the judge makes his final decision.''

''Yes.''

''If I agree to stay on as their nanny until then, will you stop talking about this marriage business?''

''Probably not.''

She laughed brokenly. ''You're relentless.''

''Usually. Until I get what I want.''

''And you want me.''

His eyes darkened. ''Oh, yeah.''

''I meant as your wife.''

''The only way the nuns would have approved.''

''I *meant* to…because of the children.''

''I couldn't have said it better.''

Her lips tightened. ''Don't tease.''

''Sorry.''

He didn't look it. He looked hard. Relentless. Only when her gaze was caught in his did she see more. His edginess. His tension.

It would be so easy to tell him yes. To just agree. To go along with the flow. And it would be so very, very wrong. He didn't know who she was. If he did, he would have every right to boot her right out onto the street.

''I'll stay on as their nanny until you're ready to leave Fisher Falls,'' she said shakily. ''But if you're set on finding a wife, you'll have to look elsewhere.''

"You'll change your mind."

"No. I won't."

He smiled faintly and finally, *finally,* began buttoning his shirt. "Time will tell, won't it?"

Chapter Eleven

"Look at this. You're not going to believe it!"

At Darby's outraged gasp, Garrett looked up from his computer, barely managing to move the keyboard out of the way before she slapped the newspaper down on it. Twenty minutes ago she'd been cleaning up the kitchen after breakfast. Now she looked poleaxed. "What don't you believe?"

"Look at it!"

He glanced briefly at the section heading. The Leisure section. "I quit reading the comics after Charles Schultz died. No more Snoopy."

She made an impatient noise and jabbed her finger against the paper. "This."

This was a grainy long-distance shot of a man in a dark suit and a woman in a floaty white dress. "That's us," he said, surprised. "At the courthouse yesterday.'' He'd had his arm around her shoulder because she'd still been shaky from the elevator.

"Read the caption," she gritted.

Wedding Bells Ringing? Millionaire developer Garrett Cullum escorted his mystery woman in white from the Fisher Falls courthouse yesterday, quashing hopes of wishful young women everywhere.

"Wishful women everywhere," he repeated, amused.

"It's not funny."

He shrugged. "It's a gossip column. That's what they do. Gossip."

"People have *seen* that."

"Around here, maybe. But the *Fisher Falls Gazette* isn't exactly the *New York Times*." The photo didn't carry a credit, he noticed. "Just think. Some person without a life was actually sitting outside the courthouse with a camera. Probably in the park across the street, from the looks of it."

"What if it gets picked up. You know? One of the news wires?"

"It's a poor-quality photo from a backwater town in northern Minnesota. I think the world will live if it isn't."

"Garrett!"

He pushed the paper aside and looked at her. "Why are you panicking over this? Nobody pays attention to gossip columns."

She flopped her hands impatiently. "Yes, they do. 'Millionaire developer'? What's that about?"

He shrugged. "I do own G&G Construction and

Development. And my bank account is fairly healthy these days."

"Great. More jokes."

"My banker smiles every time I see him." Her skin was paler than normal. "You really have a thing against reporters and such." Vultures, she'd called them.

"I just like my privacy. Why on earth didn't you say you were well off?"

"Sorry," he said shortly. "I'd have let you run a credit report on me if I knew it mattered so much. You're not the only one who prizes their privacy. Which is why I choose to keep a low profile." He leaned back in his chair, watching her closely. "But I'm not turning gray over one blurry photo. You're not even identified, Darby."

"Thank God for small favors," she muttered.

Since they'd returned to the house yesterday, there hadn't been one moment when Darby hadn't had one or more of the kids attached to her hip or wrapped around her leg. If he had to make a guess, she'd been deliberately avoiding him. And now she was practically tearing out her hair over a blurry newspaper photo. To say she was regretting what had happened the day before was putting it mildly.

"Obviously the notion of being witnessed in my company is on a par with being cornered by a reporter for you." He pushed the paper back toward her and moved his computer keyboard into place.

Darby struggled with the panic that threatened her until she wanted to scream at it and Garrett's logic that told her she really was overreacting.

Then he shoved away from his desk and strode past her toward the front door. "I'm going to work. Stop worrying,'' he said flatly. ''Your face is hardly visible with that enormous hat you were wearing. Nobody'll recognize you.''

He went out the front door, leaving her staring after him. He was annoyed.

No. He was hurt. She'd hurt him.

Regret came swift and hard, and she rushed out the door after him, but he was already driving down the street in his truck.

She might have left her old life behind, but she was still piling one mess right on top of another. Sighing, she went back inside, just in time to rescue the ringing telephone from Regan, who had a habit of answering the phone and promptly hanging up on the caller.

''Hello?''

''You go and get married without even telling me?''

Georgie. ''I'm not married.'' She hastily caught Keely from climbing into the cold, empty fireplace and redirected her toward the soft blocks that Bridget and Tad were playing with.

''So what was that picture in the paper all about, then?''

''I told him that people read gossip columns.'' She sat on the edge of the couch. Keely turned her attention to Darby's shoelaces. ''You must be having a good day.''

''You're avoiding the question. But I'll let you, for now. I told Karl to swallow that pain medicine himself. If I'm really going to have only a limited number of days left, I'm choosing to be lucid for them. Bring the children over, dear. Spend the day here. I'll have Cook fix all your favorites for lunch. Please.''

''I'm currently without wheels. My car won't start, and Garrett's already gone to work.''

An excuse that mattered little to Georgie. And a few minutes later Darby hung up the phone. She'd never been able to say no to Georgie.

"I remember Garrett's mother. She was a pretty one." Georgie had talked Darby into fixing her hair, and she was looking at the results in a gilded hand mirror. "Yes, that looks quite nice, dear. Where was I?" She handed the mirror to Darby. "Oh, yes. Bonnie Cullum. She worked for the Carson family, as did her mother before her. I always thought it odd how she kept working for the Carson family even after, well, after she had the baby."

Darby glanced out the window as she put the mirror back on Georgie's dresser. On the grass below she could see Karl and Lucinda—Cook—playing with the children. "What happened to her?" She felt almost guilty asking Georgie for information. But her aunt had brought up the subject all on her own.

"You know, I was never sure, or maybe I'm so old now that I've forgotten." Georgie's bright gaze settled on Darby. "I'd heard that her death affected Caldwell Carson very deeply," she went on. "Now there's a man who hasn't had a happy life. I don't like to speak ill of the dead, but his daughter...that Elise. She was quite a piece of work. A more spoiled woman I'd never met. Unless it was her mother, Caldwell's wife. I can't imagine either of them bringing Caldwell much more than misery."

It was a far different picture than Garrett would have painted. "Do you know him well? Mayor Carson?"

"Well enough, I suppose. He took over his family's business after his father practically ran it into the ground. Drink, you know. And it was a good thing he did. This town needed the employment. But I suspect he sacrificed his own happiness in the process. Now, stop watching and worrying out the window. The children will be just fine with Karl and Cook. Sit down here with me.''

Darby swallowed. They'd had lunch. They'd primped with powder and pots of expensive makeup. They'd styled hair and Darby had even read aloud from the latest spy thriller Georgie was reading. But now it was time to face the music. Georgie-style. She sat in the chair next to the lace-draped bed. ''Are you sure you don't want a manicure, too? I'd be happy to give you one.''

''Stop fussing, dear. You're worse than Molly Myers. She came by yesterday to visit. I understand she was none too pleased when you told her you were not returning to your job at Smiling Faces.''

''She did you a favor by hiring me in the first place. I think she was mostly worried that I'd expect her to hold the position open for me. When I, um, need it again.''

Georgie looked at her for a long moment. ''And you don't plan to need it again. Does that mean you're ready to go back home now? Or does it mean there's more to that newspaper photo than speculation? I'd love to think you'd be staying in Fisher Falls because you'd fallen in love with a man like Garrett Cullum.''

''You know I'm not interested in marriage.'' Particularly the kind Garrett had proposed. ''I just work for the man.''

Georgie's lips thinned impatiently. ''I don't have time left on this earth to listen to nonsense. Karl saw you and Garrett in the gatehouse yesterday. He was gathering leaves for me. You know how I like the scent of the outdoors in here with me. He says you two looked quite, ah, cozy.''

Darby's skin heated. ''I'm sure Karl exaggerated.''

''Pooh. Garrett is a real man, Darby dear. Nothing like that mealymouthed Bryan. The only time that pup ever stood up to anything was when he left you standing at the altar. Now, I know you were embarrassed by that, but really, dear, it was for the best. Wasn't it?''

''I was a little more than embarrassed, Georgie.''

Her aunt's expression softened. ''I know. You were so attached to his children. But don't forget. I remember when you and Bryan first started seeing each other.''

''At the Schute Clinic,'' Darby murmured. ''You were there for weeks. Making sure your endowment was being properly used.'' Despite Georgie's age and declining health, she'd been a holy terror when she'd arrived at the acclaimed pediatric clinic, cowing doctors and nurses and administrators alike.

''I was there to see *you*, darling. I know how hard your father made it for you to get through nursing school. My nephew is terribly hardheaded about some things. But you did it, and you found your own place at the Schute Clinic with no help from any of us. I was so proud of you. Every child who passed through the doors on your shift loved you. I was delighted when you told me about Bryan.

''But then I saw you two together. And, well, Darby dear, there was just no *passion* between you. And I must say, sometimes there is just nothing more important than a grand, sweeping passion. The kiss and touch of a man that makes you forget your own name.

The kind that goes hand in hand with love you never expected to find.''

Her eyes seemed lost in memories. Then she focused point-blank on Darby. ''You know I'm delighted that you came here to me when you felt you had to get away. This big old place will be yours once I'm gone, after all. But you really are so much stronger than you think you are, darling. I hope you're finally beginning to realize that.''

She tutted impatiently. ''I could *almost* feel guilty for not admitting that you were here, safe and sound, when your father called, looking for you. Quite *obviously* he didn't believe me, or his security man wouldn't have been in Fisher Falls. But then he and I have been on opposite sides of the fence his whole life.''

''Because he's one of the few people in this world who doesn't agree with everything you say,'' Darby pointed out dryly. Her father and Georgie were very much alike in that regard. It was no wonder they couldn't agree on anything.

''Well, he's been an overprotective fool where you're concerned.''

''As long as nobody knows who I really am, Daddy has no need to worry. Nobody has any interest in the very ordinary Darby White.''

''From the looks of that photo in the paper this morning, Garrett Cullum has plenty of interest in the woman his arm was around, regardless of her name.''

''He just needs someone to help his custody case against Mayor Carson.''

''Are you sure that's all?''

Darby sat back in the chair, wrapping her arms around herself, not letting herself think beyond that.

"It doesn't matter, in the end. Three people, including his sister, died because of me."

"They died because of an automobile accident," Georgie corrected gently. She leaned her head back against her pillows and sighed tiredly. "You've always been too hard on yourself, dear. Always taking responsibility for what other people have done. Do you ever wonder why two cars would collide like that on a perfectly clear day on an otherwise quiet corner?"

Darby knew she should go to bed. Bridget had a habit of waking at 3:00 a.m., an hour that came far too quickly. It wasn't as if she wasn't tired. Their visit to Georgie had gone as smoothly as it could go, considering the planning it took just to travel down the street with five kids, much less go out for the entire afternoon. But it was all worth it, just for the smile on Georgie's face when they'd arrived.

Yet now, with the children bathed and finally all asleep, Darby found herself sitting in Garrett's swivel chair, staring at his computer.

It had a dedicated phone line, she knew. Garrett did a lot of work on-line. She settled her hand over the mouse. The screensaver—a whirling eddy of greens and blues—disappeared and there it was. The little picture that, if she clicked on it, would connect her to the Internet.

She could send an e-mail to her brother. Let him know she was okay. Just a quick hi and bye. He'd certainly pass on the message to their father.

Her fingers curled and she sat back. No. She wasn't ready yet. Maybe someday. When she knew that she could stand firmly on her own two feet and not let them take over her life again.

She wasn't that strong yet. If she were, she wouldn't have been so terribly tempted to fall in with Garrett's proposal.

Her pulse quickened. Oh, had she been tempted.

And sitting here in his chair, in his den that was the only room in the house that was simply, purely, *him,* she felt that temptation flood through her all over again.

Not even Bryan, whom Darby had still loved after she'd learned that their engagement had been arranged by her father, had made her feel the way Garrett did.

When Bryan had suggested they wait to make love until after the wedding ceremony, she'd been touched by his romantic, old-fashioned chivalry. Only afterward, after her life had blown apart, did she realize why he'd always been so circumspect.

As Georgie had observed. There had been no *passion.*

She left the den and the temptation of the computer and went out into the backyard, sitting on the step in the dwindling twilight. She propped her chin in her hands, listening to the sound of the crickets and the low rumblings from the sky.

Another thunderstorm was brewing.

Garrett hadn't come home for dinner. There'd been no message on the answering machine about his plans.

He'd been supportive and she'd behaved like an idiot. All over a photo that, in all likelihood, wouldn't be noticed by anyone beyond the city limits of Fisher Falls.

She pushed to her feet, nodding to the neighbor man who was standing on a ladder next door replacing a light bulb. He waved and said he hoped they got some rain out of all that noise tonight. She smiled and agreed and told him good-night before she went back inside the house.

Something so simple. One neighbor talking to another. But until she'd found refuge in Fisher Falls, it was something that Darby had never before experienced.

And with each passing day, the thought of giving it up again only grew more painful.

Garrett stood in the dark house, staring at the still shadow on the couch. If Darby wanted to sleep on that thing, who was he to stop her?

He got himself a cold beer, then went into the den, replacing the clothes that had gotten wet from the rainstorm for a pair of old sweatpants. He flipped through the mail that Darby had left on his desk. He drank his beer halfway down.

Maybe she hadn't intended to fall asleep down here. The couch was too damned lumpy to get a decent night's sleep. He ought to know. The pullout in the den wasn't much better.

He'd go wake her. Then she could go upstairs. Someone should be making use of that brand-new mattress up there.

He set the long-neck on the desk and went out to the living room. She was curled into a tight ball. As if, even in sleep, she needed to keep the world at bay.

"Who are you, Darby White?" he murmured.

She slept on.

Cursing himself for a fool, he leaned over and slid his arms beneath her gathering up the ghostly white robe twisted around her and lifting her easily against him. She was so incredibly leggy that he was continually surprised at how small she really was.

She sighed and turned her face trustingly into his shoulder. Her breath whispered over his skin. He swore under his breath and headed for the stairs. They were so narrow he had to turn sideways to carry her up and even then he managed to crack his elbow against the wall.

"Mmmm." Darby's arm glided over his arm, up his chest, around his neck. "You're home," she whispered huskily.

Garrett grimaced. She was probably dreaming about the idiot ex-fiancé. The door to his bedroom was ajar, and he nudged it wider, carrying her over to the bed.

He shifted her in his arms, yanking back the covers before lowering her to the sheet. Her hands linked behind his neck and she made a protesting little sound. A sexy little sound that went straight to his gut.

"Come on, Darby," he murmured in a low voice. He looked at the cribs. The babies were all soundly sleeping. He wanted to keep it that way. "Time for bed."

He unlatched her slender fingers from his neck, only she twined her fingers with his, drawing their hands toward her, making that same sound again.

God. He was a glutton for punishment.

The belt of her robe was doing a rotten job of holding the robe together. And the silky nightgown underneath did a rotten job of not clinging to her lean curves. And the nightlight she'd plugged into the wall did an excellent job of illuminating it all.

He slid his hands out from hers, telling himself that he wasn't noticing the jutting curve of her breast against his knuckles.

"Garrett."

Her velvety voice whispered to him so faintly he wondered if he'd made it up in his head. He lowered his head, still leaning across the bed. *Get a grip.* He started to straighten, but her arm slid across the cool sheet toward him, her palm turned trustingly upward.

"I'm sorry," she whispered, just as quietly. Her eyes were open. Just.

"For what?"

Her head moved faintly. "Everything."

The word sighed over him. Knowing he'd be smarter to let it go, his knee settled on the bed, anyway. She turned toward him. Smoothly. Warmly. Lifting her head toward his. Pressing her soft lips against his.

Want, never far when she was near, settled deep inside him. He kissed her. One kiss wouldn't kill them.

Her mouth parted, her tongue shyly flicking.

One kiss only was gonna kill him.

He pushed at her robe with the faulty, lackadaisical tie belt. She twisted and kicked it away. Then her arms, satin smooth, strong, female, wrapped around him and he was only too willing to follow.

He rolled, pulling her over him, filling his hands with her slender hips, running his palm beneath the hem, finding another scrap of satin beneath, then just the warm sleek curve of her back. She arched against his hand, supple as a cat. Her fingers flexed against his scalp, her breath becoming his.

"Your hair is wet," she murmured.

"The rain." The stringy things that held up her nightgown slipped so easily away as he drew the fabric up. Over her head.

She sat up and the nightlight gleamed like gold over

her ivory skin. He could see the pulse beating in her neck as her arms crossed over herself. Her eyes were dark pools in the pale oval of her face.

The raging fire inside him eased in the face of her shy modesty. He sat up against the pillows and gently took her hands in his, uncrossing her arms. Her fingers curled, unsteady. "I want to see you," he murmured. She was beautiful. He pressed his mouth to her collarbone. Rubbed his fingers over her slender torso. Dipped into the gentle valley between her breasts. Grazed over the tight nipples.

She trembled wildly against him as he tasted each curve. So sweet. So creamy. So—

"*Mamaaaaaaa!*"

The sobbing scream jerked his head back. He swallowed a curse as Darby suddenly scrambled off him, yanking on her nightgown, throwing her robe over her shoulders. "Reid," she mumbled and darted out of the room.

Garrett thumped his head against the wall behind him. A crying kid. Better than a cold shower.

He wondered how parents ever managed.

He could hear Darby's low voice murmuring to Reid. Then one of the triplets started crying.

He rolled out of bed and stepped over to the cribs. It was Bridget. Sitting there, rubbing her eyes, her mouth pouting as she cried softly.

Then she held up her hands to him, clearly expecting him to do something. In the other room he could hear Reid, still upset.

Garrett reached into the crib and picked her up. She snuggled close against him, her crying miraculously stopped. She babbled nonsensically.

"Yeah," Garrett muttered, carrying her with him downstairs before she managed to wake up her brother and sister with her chatter. "That's a woman for you. Always giving a guy a hard time."

Chapter Twelve

Darby woke with a start. She was lying in Reid's bed, where she'd fallen asleep with him, and sunlight filled the room.

There was no sign of either Reid or Regan.

She blinked, feeling positively blurry in the head, and climbed out of the narrow bed. The bedside clock in the other bedroom told her it was nearly ten in the morning, and shock propelled her downstairs.

The triplets were safe and sound, dressed in colorful shorts and shirts and contained within the safe zone of the living room thanks to the baby gates she'd borrowed from Smiling Faces.

Keely was standing all on her own, and Darby smiled, delightedly kissing the tot on the head. Then she stepped over the gate into the kitchen to find Regan and Reid sitting at the table, both studiously drawing on big sheets of white paper. Drafting paper, she realized, and finally focused on Garrett, who was also sitting at the table.

Her entire body went into a slow burn. "I'm... sorry," she fumbled. "I overslept."

"We managed. Surprisingly enough." He set aside the sheaf of papers he'd been studying, placing them on the counter where curious little hands couldn't reach. "Carmel has the office well in hand. She loves to lord it over me and tell me that I'm basically unnecessary."

"You're not."

His smile was brief. "I need to talk to you."

Her stomach twisted. She'd practically thrown herself at him last night. Right there in the same bedroom as the sleeping babies. No matter what kind of arrangement he'd proposed with her, behavior like that was simply outrageous. He had every reason to be appalled.

He was standing by the back door, his expression unreadable. And her stomach did more than twist. It seemed to fall right down to her feet. Lower. Through the floor. "What is it?"

He drew her outside, where the sun shone brightly, all evidence of the rain from the night before gone. "I got a call this morning," he said quietly. His eyes were gentle. Utterly serious. Her heart simply stopped.

"My father—"

He frowned a little, shaking his head. "A guy named Karl."

Sudden tears lodged in her throat.

"They had to take Georgie to the hospital last night."

"No." She shook her head. "I was with her yesterday. She was good. We had lunch. Crab salad for us and chicken fingers for the kids.'' Her voice broke.

''I'm sorry, sweetheart. I know you're very close to her.''

Darby brushed her fingers over her cheeks. ''I have to go see her. She'll be mad if she finds out I was crying. Tell me it's a waste of good water.''

''That sounds like the Georgina Vansant I know. The one who offered me a job when no one else would.''

She managed a shaky smile. But it didn't last. ''I don't want to lose her, Garrett. I know it's going to happen one day, but I'm not ready yet,'' she whispered. ''I'm sorry. I shouldn't complain. Not after your sister…and all.''

He pulled her against him, tucking her head beneath his chin. ''I wish I could tell you that losing Elise hurt me this much. That there was that much caring between us. But there wasn't. And I think that's what hurts the most.''

Darby caught back a sob.

She felt him kiss her forehead. ''Georgie is wrong about one thing,'' he said gruffly. ''It's not a waste of water.''

Her arms crept around him, and he held her while she cried. Then, once she collected herself and got dressed, he loaded everyone into his truck and drove Darby to the hospital himself.

Unfortunately there wasn't much any of them could do when they arrived. Georgie was in the Intensive Care Unit, and Darby was allowed to visit her for only a few minutes once each hour. Darby spent her few minutes with her aunt reading aloud to her. Georgie was unconscious, but Darby knew that her aunt was somehow, somewhere, listening.

Halfway through the second hour, the children were going mad from being confined in the waiting room. The only saving grace had been that the seven of them were the only ones in the room, so they'd been free to be as noisy and rambunctious as Darby and Garrett could stand.

But now Darby caught Keely from crawling out of the waiting room and popped her back in the stroller with her brother and sister.

"They need lunch," Darby told Garrett. She'd been so panicked over her aunt, she hadn't thought to make sure the supply of cereal inside the diaper bag was enough. "I'll just have to come back and visit Georgie later tonight. Maybe after the children are in bed."

He shook his head and nudged her hands away from the padded stroller handle. "You don't want to leave," he said. "I can see it on your face. I'll take them home now. When you're ready, give me a call and I'll come back and pick you up."

"I don't want to make more work for you."

"Why don't you let me worry about that."

"Garrett—"

He brushed his thumb over her lips. "Everyone should have a friend as true as you," he murmured.

His easy support made her want to cry. There was so much that wasn't true about her, and she hated that as much as she hated the fear that had been motivating her for months now.

She caught his hand between hers, noticing the way his sun-bronzed skin looked in comparison to her pallor. "I'm not just her friend," she admitted after a long moment. "Georgie is my great-aunt, Garrett."

His expression didn't change. "Okay."

"You don't want to know why I didn't mention it before?"

"Was there a good reason?"

She swallowed. "I...needed to get away," she faltered. "From everything."

"That ended up being our good luck."

"Oh, Garrett."

He glanced at the children. Regan was watching them openly. Reid was picking at a loose thread on his shirt. "Darby, I know I'm not the best at some things, but...if you want to talk. You know." His mouth twisted crookedly. "Hell, you already know most of my secrets now. Least I can do is return the favor."

She chewed her lip. "Garrett, I—" She couldn't do it. She couldn't tell him, right there in front of the five children, that she'd been responsible for their parents' death. She was the absolute worst kind of coward.

"Miss White?" One of the nurses appeared in the wide doorway of the waiting room. "Mrs. Vansant is coming around. She's asking for you."

Darby's mouth parted. She looked back at Garrett, unbearably torn.

"Go on, Darby." He lifted his chin toward the door and told Regan and Reid to gather up the magazines they'd scattered about. "Call when you want to head home."

Home. All she'd ever wanted and the one thing she'd never seemed to really have.

"Thank you," she whispered. Then she stretched up and pressed a quick, trembling kiss against his lips, before following the nurse back to Georgie's bedside.

* * *

Three days later Garrett sat in the kitchen of his dumpy little rental house and scooped goopy chunks of pears into three hungry mouths, and wondered what the hell had become of his life.

What had happened to the guy whose house—designed and built mostly by his own hands—had won architectural and design awards? The guy who did deals; who traveled around the country on a moment's notice; who enjoyed the company and charms of tall, curvy blondes; who answered only to himself and liked it that way?

Keely patted his cheek with her little hand and talked nonsensically. Tad was kicking his legs, grinning and displaying the sharp edges of two shiny new teeth. Regan was picking up the sipper cup that Bridget had thrown to the kitchen floor. Reid was standing on the chair seat behind Garrett, sprawled over his back like a wet blanket as he seemed to find great interest in the shape of Garrett's right ear.

The phone rang, and before Garrett could disentangle Reid from him, Regan bounced over to the wall phone. "Regan, wait—"

Too late. Regan picked it up. "Hello!" she greeted cheerfully, then promptly pushed the phone back on the cradle. She turned around and beamed at Garrett, then bent down and picked up Bridget's sipper cup when it went sailing again.

Garrett shook his head and laughed wryly. He guessed if it was important, the caller would try again.

He didn't know how to describe his life now, except to say it was *definitely* different. And, honest to God, he couldn't wait for Darby to once again be more than an in-and-out visitor in this new, unrecognizable life of his. Since Georgie seemed to be improving, he hoped that'd be soon.

Which just went to show what a selfish soul he really was.

He finished feeding the triplets, which wasn't as much of a disaster as some of his attempts, then cleaned them up some before sticking them on the floor in the living room where an assortment of baby gates kept them corralled with their toys and away from hazards. Then he turned to the two older ones. "Bath time," he announced.

Reid yelled and ran out of the room.

"I don't want soap in my eyes no more," Regan said, her smile gone as she warily eyed him.

Garrett grimaced. "I don't want that anymore, either," he assured. When he'd inadvertently let shampoo suds drip into her face the evening before, Regan had let the entire neighborhood know with her crying just how much it stung.

"Darby doesn't get soap in my eyes."

"I know, peaches." Garrett blew out a breath. "Tell you what. If Darby gets home from the hospital in the next hour, then you can have her. But if she doesn't, then we'll have to muddle through together."

Satisfied, Regan ran off, yelling for her brother. Garrett turned to the kitchen and restored it to some semblance of order. Then he attacked the laundry that was threatening to take over the minuscule laundry room. Darby had done a good portion of it, and there were neat stacks of clean, dry and folded clothes, along with the two baskets of stuff from the toddlers.

It seemed as if they went through a drawerful of items per kid each day.

There was no point in grumbling over it, though.

Staring at it wasn't going to make it go away. So he dumped some detergent in the washing machine and shoved it full to bursting, then grabbed up an armful of the clean things and carried them upstairs. He didn't even realize he had a handful of Darby's clothes until he'd shoved the top half of the piles into what he hoped were the right drawers in the kids' dressers.

One minute he was holding miniature socks, T-shirts and shorts and the next, he was holding a bundle of filmy, lacy things. He stood in the master bedroom, staring at the lingerie in his hands and damn near broke out in a sweat. It was crazy. He was not some pimple-faced teenager, faced with his first sight of a woman's panties and bra.

Garrett's fingers closed around the frothy, delicate things. His gaze fell on the bed that Darby slept in each night.

Then he heard the latch of the screen door from downstairs and Darby's sexy, husky voice as she greeted the toddlers. He strode around the bed and yanked open the drawers of the small chest there that he figured Darby was using for her own, since the other dresser in the room was filled with baby stuff. He started to shove the lingerie into the second drawer, thinking that the sooner he got out of there, the better.

But the colorful magazine cover inside the drawer caught his eye, and he went still for a moment.

Her hairstyle was different, but there was no mistaking that color. Very aware of the sound of Darby moving around downstairs, Garrett dropped the bundle of lingerie into the drawer. The satin and lace bits covered the magazine, and Garrett almost wished he hadn't seen it at all. Because even as one puzzle piece was fitted into place, it seemed to make him more aware than ever of the other pieces still missing.

Standing at the base of the stairs, Darby looked up the staircase. "Garrett? Are you— Oh, there you are."

He'd appeared on the landing, looking particularly tall and broad from her angle below. "You're earlier than I expected," he said as he started down the stairs. "How's Georgie tonight?"

"Pretty good, actually. She's scheduled for surgery tomorrow morning. Once she decided she wanted to go for it, the surgeon saw no reason to delay." She looked at him. She would like to rest her head against that wide chest. Instead, she went into the living room, busying herself with straightening the cushions on the couch and adjusting the skewed lampshade.

"That's good, right?"

"Well, yes. Georgie isn't young, of course. But her surgeon is optimistic. And Georgie is determined." She stepped over one of the baby gates and sat down on the floor to lift Tad into her lap. He gave her a toothy grin, and Darby's heart suddenly felt lighter.

Feeling the steady weight of Garrett's gaze, she glanced up at him. Then hesitated. "Is something wrong?"

"No."

Whatever he said, she could guess. "You should have found someone else to watch the kids," she told him, even though the notion made her feel empty inside. "The past three days, I know I've barely been here. That's certainly not what you hired me for."

He sat down on the arm of the couch and stretched out his legs, his eyes never leaving her face. "When are you going to get it through your head that I don't want to hire somebody else? Nothing's changed," he seemed to stress the words, "as far as I'm concerned. I want you to marry me. Remember?"

As if she could forget. "Garrett, I've already told you that I can't."

He lifted his hand. "Let's not get into that just now," he suggested smoothly. "So your aunt was in good form today, then?"

Darby kissed Tad's head and let the squirming boy go. She folded her hands in her lap and looked at them. Since Darby had admitted to him that Georgie was her great-aunt, he hadn't once referred to her that way. It struck her as…odd. But then, the entire situation they were living in was hardly the norm.

She looked up as Regan and Reid came racing down the stairs, chasing each other and whooping at the tops of their voices. At least the children seemed normal at the moment.

It did little to ease her conscience, however.

"Yes, she was." She focused on Garrett's comment about Georgie. "She made me promise not to wear white tomorrow if I 'insist' on being at the hospital while she's in surgery."

"Oh, yeah?"

"She doesn't want me reminding her too much of angels."

"You do seem a little angelic," he murmured. "Look at the way you've helped save us."

Darby shook her head. "I haven't."

His lips tilted. "So. What does she prefer you to wear? Red?"

"Well. Yes, actually." She felt silly admitting it. "How did you know?"

He shrugged easily. "Seems like a Georgie color. Do you even own anything that isn't white or tan?"

Darby waved her hand at the narrow garment bag she'd left by the front door. "I scrounged up a dress from my closet at the gatehouse. She also made me promise to personally go by her house tomorrow and check on her houseplants. Since she's been in the hospital, there hasn't been a need for her staff to go the house, and she's pretty attached to her ferns and such."

"What time is the surgery?"

"Nine."

"I'll go with you."

Darby's throat tightened. "I—" She looked at him and the automatic refusal of his offer died, unsaid. "Thank you." Then, because of the steady way his mossy-green eyes kept watching her, she plucked Bridget off the floor and stood. "Diaper time," she announced.

She stepped over the gate, waiting for Garrett to move his outstretched legs, but he didn't. She moistened her lips and stepped over them, as well, making the mistake of glancing at his face as she did so.

Her breath stalled. She nearly tripped. He put out one long arm, catching her hip, steadying her and Bridget.

"Garrett—" She didn't know what she wanted to say.

His gaze dropped to her mouth. The fingers on her hip flexed. She felt herself leaning just a bit closer to him.

Closer.

The phone rang and Darby jerked back, catching her breath. Garrett muttered something about "racing Regan" under his breath as he straightened and strode into his den.

She heard him answer the phone. Then the low tone of his voice. Business. Naturally he'd have to handle a lot of business at home. In the evenings; whenever he could fit it in around caring for the children the way he'd been doing the past few days.

She blew out a long breath and focused on the tot in her arms. "Your uncle is a good guy," she murmured as she carried Bridget upstairs for a fresh diaper.

When she came back down, Garrett was still on his phone call.

It was just as well. She needed to remember that she *wasn't* Garrett's devoted fiancée. She was nanny to his fearsome five and the fact that she couldn't look at him without thinking of the night he'd carried her up to bed was something she'd just have to get over.

She settled Bridget back on the floor with the other two and rounded up Regan and Reid for their baths and bedtime story.

Once that was accomplished and she'd settled the babies down after snuggles and a last bottle, she headed for the laundry that she'd left early that morning.

Only the stacks she'd expected to see still sitting on top of the dryer were gone. She opened up the washing machine to find a wet load waiting. She transferred it to the dryer and turned to find Garrett standing behind her.

She stepped back, bumping against the appliances behind her. "You startled me."

"Sorry. I put the clothes and stuff away already."

"Oh. Right. Thanks."

"Here." He held out a wad of bills. "Your pay."

"I've barely done anything to earn it since Georgie

went into the hospital. You've even arranged for that second truck that I've been using. I don't think I should accept it.''

He pushed the money into her hand, despite her protest. ''Unless you're ready to call a justice of the peace and be done with it, you'll accept it.''

She rolled the cash into a tube, closing her fingers around it. ''Garrett, this marriage thing, it's not going to happen.''

''Why?''

''We've already been through this.''

''You can do better than us, I know.''

''No! No. You know that's not what I think. Garrett, you're a good man. A…decent man. Any woman would be lucky to have you and the children for her own, but—''

''Not you.''

''Yes. No.'' She shook her head, feeling overwhelmed and confused and sad. ''I thought you didn't want to get into this.''

''I didn't while the kids were right there. But they're all in bed now.''

''Which is probably where I should be, too,'' she said hurriedly. ''I'll finish this stuff up in the morning. It's just towels and things. It won't harm them being in the dryer until then. It shuts off automatically, you know.''

''Are you afraid of me?''

Her jaw dropped. ''Afraid? No. Should I be?''

''Then why are you acting like a long-tailed cat in a roomful of rocking chairs?''

She gave a breathless laugh. ''My father uses that expression.''

''Does he?'' Garret stepped closer. ''If you're not

afraid, then why can I see your pulse beating in your throat?''

She lifted her hand, pressing it against that betraying sign. "Look, Garrett. About the other…that night. I shouldn't have—''

"Why not? We're adults. I want you. You want me. What's more simple than that? I'd rather this place had another bedroom for us to put the cribs in, but we'll be more careful next time.''

Her skin heated. "Next…time.''

He cupped her chin and raised it. He kissed her lips, gently, tantalizingly. "Next time. You know this is where we're headed, Darby.''

"But I can't marry you.''

"Yes, you can." His words were a whisper over her mouth. "It'll be fine, Darby. I'll take care of everything.''

She sighed, sinking so easily into his kiss. So seductive, so tantalizing. Making her want more and more.

I'll take care of everything.

His words finally sank into her muddled brain. "No.'' She wedged her hands between them and pushed him away. "No! I don't need you to take care of everything. I don't want someone running my life for me. I want to make my own decisions, my own choices, my own mistakes!''

She stared at him, shocked at the words that had tumbled from her mouth.

"We all do, Darby,'' Garrett said quietly, as if he could see straight to her soul and recognized all the fears that drove her. "I meant that I'd take care of finding a justice of the peace. But whether or not we find a JP before or after makes no difference to me.''

There was no mistaking his implication. "You seem to think that's a forgone conclusion. Our, ah…"

"Making love," he supplied. "Sooner or later, Darby, it is."

She wanted to disagree. But the denial wouldn't quite come to her lips. So she just stood there, feeling awkward and much too aware of his appeal.

He watched her for a long moment. Long enough to make her brush her fingers through her hair. Long enough to make her wonder if she'd buttoned her blouse crookedly.

"You've been under a lot of stress," he finally said, and something about the way he said it made tears suddenly burn behind her eyes.

"That was Hayden on the phone earlier," he went on. "I've got to go into the office for a while. I'll be late getting back. Don't leave for the hospital in the morning without me. And," he brushed his thumb over her lips when she started to speak, "I'll arrange for child care, too. Not that I think you're incapable of doing it yourself," he added with a faint smile. "Okay?"

She managed a smile herself and nodded. She even managed to hold her composure together when he ducked his head and pressed a hard, fast kiss to her lips.

But once he was gone, she slid to the floor in a quivering mess and pressed her forehead to her knees.

The man sure knew how to kiss. It was enough to make her forget her own name.

Chapter Thirteen

Darby walked through the central corridor of Georgie's grand old house carrying the filled watering can. She tipped it gingerly over each potted plant. The last thing she wanted to do was drown one of Georgie's precious green things.

She looked over at Garrett, who was running his hand across an inlaid door, his expression appreciative. True to his word, he'd driven Darby to the hospital. He'd visited with Georgie before she was rolled out of her room. He hadn't left Darby's side for more than a few minutes at a time since.

She tipped and watered. "How was Carmel faring with the children when you phoned?"

"Better than she admits, I suspect." He moved to her side of the wide hallway, touching the wall, crouching down to look at something near the floor.

"Well. It was very nice of her to stay with the children while Georgie had her surgery.'' She moistened her lips. ''I do appreciate your support today. But I really can handle watering Georgie's plants by myself.'' She jiggled the oversize, plastic watering can.

He stood and took the can from her. ''Did they teach you these manners in finishing school?''

She jerked, startled. ''What?''

He grinned slightly. ''You are pretty polished.''

Darby rolled her eyes. Since the watering can weighed a small ton, she let him take it and led him into the sunroom where she sat down, nudging off her shoes with relief. She'd have much preferred her usual tennis shoes, but with the red dress she'd worn per Georgie's instructions, they would have looked ludicrous.

Garrett poured water into the pots, and Darby, realizing she was watching him much too closely, looked beyond his dark head, through the sparkling windowpanes where the falls were visible in the distance. It looked like a rippling veil tumbling over the sheer rocks.

''Georgie's bedroom upstairs has the same view as this room,'' she murmured. ''She loves it. So do I.''

Garrett set the can down and closed his hands over the back of her shoulders, staying her when she jumped a little. ''Her surgery went well. She'll be back talking to her plants and admiring the view before you know it.''

''Yes.'' Darby smiled faintly. ''And ordering Karl and Cook and everyone else around.'' His massaging fingers felt much too good, and she shifted away. Stood. ''Speaking of orders, there are probably a dozen plants upstairs, too. She'll have my head if I neglect a single one of them.''

"Relax. I'll finish watering the plants. I've wanted to explore this great old place since I was a kid. It'll give me a chance." He shrugged out of his black suit coat and dropped it haphazardly on a chair, picking up the watering can again as he left the room.

Darby watched him go, chewing the inside of her lip. She picked up his jacket, only intending to straighten it from the wrinkled heap he'd dropped it in. But the fine fabric smelled of him, and her fingers tightened around the garment. Hugging it to her, she moved blindly about the sunroom. Remembering the first time she'd come here three months ago.

Despite their family connection, Darby had never visited Georgie in Fisher Falls. She felt bad about that now. But her aunt had traveled so much. She'd always seemed to enjoy descending upon them in Kentucky, where she and Darby's father would battle over everything from the color of the sky to the price of the company stock.

Yet, when Darby had needed a place to go, Georgie had been here. Her aunt had sat right here in this very sunroom, dragging Darby's garbled tale out of her, clucking and tutting just when Darby had needed it. She'd given her a place to stay. Helped her find a job that Darby could enjoy, since she couldn't possibly find a nursing post without her name being traced.

Holding Garrett's jacket to her cheek, she leaned against the window. She'd thought she was all cried out. She'd made it through Georgie's long surgery without wasting one bit of good water. But now the tears seemed far too easy. Far too close.

She closed her eyes and wiped her cheek.

"I always figured you'd look great in red. I don't think I told you that, yet."

Embarrassed that Garrett had caught her nuzzling his jacket, she quickly smoothed it and folded it over her arm. "Why red?"

"It's about as far from your usual palette of whites as it can get."

She lay his jacket over the back of one of the rattan chairs and flicked her hand against the silk sheath she wore. "Georgie obviously agrees with that. She told me once that she wants everyone to wear red to her memorial...once she's gone." Her eyes flooded and she turned away.

"That's not going to happen anytime soon," Garrett said quietly.

She dashed her fingertips beneath her eyes and turned to face him. He'd been a rock for her, just as much as Georgie was. "I think you try to hide it, but you're a nice man, Garrett Cullum. And I couldn't have gotten through the last few days without you." She stretched up and pressed a kiss to his cheek.

He closed his wide palms over her shoulders, bare below the tiny cap sleeves, and the moment slowly stretched into infinity.

His thumbs drew gentle circles on her skin.

"Garrett—"

His lips twisted. "I know. It's not the time. Or the place. You're exhausted. But I'm...short on willpower at the moment."

Passion. Just like Georgie said. She'd approved of it, despite knowing everything there was to know about the situation. But as Darby looked at Garrett, she realized with a startling moment of clarity that it was so much more than mere passion.

It was love.

Maybe on any other day, at any other place, she

could have kept her defenses in place against the realization.

But it wasn't any other day.

It was here. And it was now. And denying the emotion that churned inside her heart, crying for release, was more than she was capable of.

"So, I think I'll head on out now," Garrett was saying wryly. "Do you want to come or stay here?"

"Why would I stay here?" she asked faintly.

"I thought maybe you'd want some time to yourself now." He reached for his jacket. "If you need a break from everything, I understand."

"What about the children?"

He looked at her for a long moment. "Nothing's changed, Darby. We'll still be there."

She drew in a shaky breath. "Actually, there is something I need."

He waited.

"Some...time to ourselves."

A muscle in his jaw flexed. "Ourselves," he repeated after a moment. "You and me."

She moistened her lips. Nodded. Her heart felt as weightless as the water must when it tumbled over the rocks, creating that beautiful, magnificent, awesome waterfall. "Unless you're averse to that."

He smiled grimly, shaking his head once. "Darby, if you and I are any more alone, you know what's going to happen."

Her chin tilted. "Yes. I know."

He studied her through narrowed eyes, and time seemed to stall. To hang like a physical thing, taut and expectant, between them. "The gatehouse?"

She shook her head. "Here. Right here. Right... now."

"Georgie—"

"Would be the first one to applaud. Trust me on that. We're alone. Karl and Lucinda won't be back until Georgie recovers and comes home."

He smiled faintly. Tossed his jacket back onto the chair. He held out his hand. "Come here."

She put her hand in his.

"You're shaking." He stepped closer.

"I've…um…" She jumped a little when his fingers grazed her neckline, then slowly, unerringly, drew the zipper down along her spine. "Um, I've never done this before," she admitted in a rush.

His fingers halted on the zipper. His eyes darkened. "Never?"

"Never." She pushed her tongue against her teeth for a moment. "Have you changed your mind now?"

He snorted softly. "Not on your life."

"Well. I might not be any good at—"

"Darby?"

"What?"

"At the risk of telling you what to do, put your mouth here—" he tapped his lips "—and be quiet."

She stretched up to him, following instructions to the letter.

Her dress slithered to the floor, and he lifted her out of it, carrying her over to the cushioned love seat. He settled her on it, then straightened, reaching for his tie.

Darby's throat tightened as he yanked it free and flicked open the buttons of his white shirt. It billowed open, harshly white against his chest. "You are a construction guy aren't you," she murmured, watching the sun-bronzed play of his muscles when he pulled the shirt off and tossed it aside.

"Yes, ma'am."

She knew she should feel decadent sitting there wearing nothing but her undies and hose, but she didn't. In fact, she was almost disappointed that he stopped undressing after his shirt.

Outside the sunroom a breeze drifted by, jingling the wind chimes that Georgie collected and hung around her house with a generous hand.

Like delighted laughter.

She tilted her head and stood. Boldly pressed herself against him, feeling more wonderfully feminine than ever before. She kissed his chest, exploring his hard muscles with her palms, going breathless all over again at the way he went still and tense when she touched him.

"Don't stop." His head curved over hers. His lips burned on her shoulder. Somewhere along the line he'd unclipped her bra and it fell, unnoticed.

His hands knew no boundaries. Hard with calluses that ought to have been out of place on a millionaire developer but weren't, they were infinitely gentle, indescribably seductive.

He pushed the cushions from the love seat onto the fluffy hand-tied rug and drew her down to them. She followed, mindless with need.

He unrolled her nylons with agonizing attention, and she watched them drift from his hand to the floor.

Then his hands settled around her ankles and she exhaled shakily. She caught the gleam of his white teeth as he smiled fiercely, utterly male, utterly aroused.

He rubbed the ache from her tender feet, seemed to find her ankles fascinating and her knees even more so.

She didn't even think to protest when he delved wickedly beneath the edge of her panties.

Again and again she restlessly reached for him only to have him elude her touch with a faint smile, his mossy-green eyes filled with intent as he taught her the wonder of a man's hands on a woman's body.

Finally his name burst from her lips, and she twisted against him in a paroxysm of need, twining her legs around his, wondering faintly when he'd gotten rid of his pants. "Please."

He kissed her deeply, finally settling hot and heavy and wonderful against the cradle of her hips. He made a low sound, deep in his throat. A sound that twined around her heart. "Open your eyes, Darby."

She did, and his hard, beautiful face filled her vision. And she felt him there. And even though she was a trained nurse, she suddenly couldn't imagine how such a thing could possibly work. "Garrett—"

He inhaled sharply, pressing his forehead against hers. "You don't know what your voice does to me," he said roughly. "Say it again."

"Garrett," she whispered.

He groaned.

She arched against him, needing more. "Garrett. Garrett. Oh." And then she could say no more.

And everything worked beautifully.

Because of him.

"It's getting late." Darby sighed as Garrett's long fingers smoothed up her spine. She pressed her cheek against his chest. "We should probably get back."

"Probably."

Neither made a single move.

Darby scooted upward, propping her chin on her hand. "We should."

"Right." His grin was slow.

Darby laughed softly.

He pulled her over him, and his warm hands cupped her hips. "So tell me why you hadn't done this before. The guy you were engaged to was a bigger jerk than I thought if he managed to keep his hands off you."

"Maybe he was a gentleman," Darby said primly.

"Something I'm definitely not."

"You're not like anyone I've ever known," she admitted honestly. "I wish—"

"What?"

She tucked her head against his neck, breathing in his scent, committing it to memory so she'd never, ever forget this moment. "I wish that we could have met under different circumstances."

"Why? We'd still be the same people."

"I know."

"For a long time, there, I wanted to be somebody other than who I was," he murmured. "Anybody other than Caldwell's bastard son. Couldn't change it when I was five or fifteen or twenty-five. Finally I quit caring."

She didn't think he had quit caring, at all. "My family is…difficult to take, too," she admitted huskily. "My parents are divorced. Mother lives in New York. Dane, my brother, gets along with her better than I do." She smiled wryly. "Actually, he gets along with all females better than anyone I know."

"Has it been a long time since you've seen them?"

"Nearly four months," she admitted. "My father…we had a disagreement. I wanted to move out. Live on my own. I'm twenty-six years old, for heaven's sake. You would have thought I'd suggested shaving my head and joining the circus.''

"Why didn't you do it anyway? Move."

"I couldn't afford it. My father used his influence with my employers, and I lost my job." She closed her eyes. She'd been furious with her father when she'd learned the truth. Dane had shrugged and told her to stop expecting the old man to change his stripes.

Dane had also thought she was crazy for remaining in the house after she'd learned the truth of her father's machinations in her engagement to Bryan.

"I was a nurse at a clinic specializing in treating pediatric cancer patients," she said.

"Sounds grim."

She shook her head. "The children I worked with had fifty times the courage that I did," she murmured. "Anyway, I had trouble finding another post." Thanks again to her father's meddling. "I think my father believed that as long as I couldn't find a job, I'd have no choice but to stay under his roof."

"Controlling."

"You have no idea," Darby murmured.

"And you ended up here, in Fisher Falls with your aunt."

"Great-aunt. On my father's side. They don't get along." Darby had a sudden thought that Garrett might mention something to Georgie. "She hasn't told him about her health or the surgery. She doesn't even like to talk about him."

"Neither do you, much," Garrett pointed out. "Do you feel a strong need to get back to the children now or not?"

Every thought flew from her mind as she looked into his hard, beautiful face. "I—"

"Good." His smile flashed as he suddenly rolled, pulling her beneath him, his intentions as obvious as the arousal he couldn't hide.

Darby twined her arms around his neck, opening her mouth to his. *I love you* hovered on the edges of her thoughts, but she managed to hold back the words.

And a few moments later she couldn't think at all.

Chapter Fourteen

"Are you sure you don't want to go to the carnival with us? It's the last day."

Garrett looked up at Darby from the pile of letters Carmel had brought by before lunch for his signature. Since Georgie's hospitalization and surgery two weeks before, he'd continued working more often at home. The elderly woman was now recuperating well in a private care center on the other side of town, where Darby visited a couple times a week.

"I can't," he said. The stab of regret he felt surprised him, and he tossed down his pen in favor of tugging Darby onto his lap. "Carmel has set up more interviews for hiring staff this afternoon, and then I've got a meeting with Hayden and the Nielson Farms folks to finalize the deal with them."

"I still find it hard to believe that Fisher Falls is

going to be the new home for a gourmet ice-cream manufacturer.''

''And G&G, who won the contract right out from under Castle Construction's nose, will get fat and happy building their plant, the new housing development, the—''

''Yeah, yeah.'' She looped her arm around his neck, resting her forehead against his. ''You millionaire developers are all alike. Brag, brag, brag. It's all you do.''

''All?'' He kissed her. Caught her soft lip between his teeth and felt her smile.

Just that easily Garrett wanted her. He put his hands on her hips and bodily lifted her until she faced him, then he lowered her once again onto his lap. His swivel chair rocked precariously.

Her eyes widened. ''Garrett! It's the middle of the afternoon.''

''So? We've got time.'' He yanked her skinny little pink top out of her shorts and pushed his hands beneath. He liked the fact that she was starting to wear some colors, almost as much as he liked the way they fit her sweet, sexy body. ''You don't have to pick up the minis from Smiling Faces for another half hour.''

''Hour,'' she corrected breathlessly.

He smiled slowly and pulled her shirt over her head, tossing it carelessly onto the desktop. ''Even better.''

''One might think that you wanted—oh, my.''

When had he ever thought her too bony for his tastes? She was perfect. Nothing went to waste on her slender body. Her coral-tipped breasts fitted his palms as if they'd been made for him. And they tasted…perfect. He lifted his head, catching the look on her face. Heavy lidded, her eyes glowed like little blue flames. "What were you saying?"

"Huh?" She blinked. Made a face at him, then somehow managed to move her legs on either side of him in the chair so that he felt as if the back of his head would blow right out. "Something wrong?" Her sexy voice was as innocent as he'd ever heard it.

He closed his hands around her hips, but she still managed to rock against him. "You're a witchy sprite."

Her lashes lowered and the tip of her tongue slowly ran along the edge of her pearly teeth. "What I was going to say, before you so…rudely…interrupted me, was that one might think you have ulterior motives for wanting the kids to start going to Smiling Faces again for a few hours each week."

"It was your idea," he reminded. "I just went along with it." He rubbed his thumb over her nipple and watched her eyes glaze.

Her throat worked, and she dug her fingertips into his shoulders. "It's good for Regan and…and Reid to, uh, be with other children their—" she groaned breathlessly "—ages. And the triplets are—"

He knew all the reasons she'd worked so hard at getting Regan and Reid to willingly return to Smiling Faces. Dealing with separation anxiety was only part. She was getting the kids prepared for when she was no longer their nanny. He understood what she was doing, but it didn't mean he had to like it. And even though he hadn't pushed the marriage thing lately, it didn't mean that he'd given up the notion.

He was incapable of love, but that didn't mean he wanted Elise's children to grow up without it the way he had. If Darby was his wife, he could make sure that didn't happen.

All good and fine thoughts, none of which were paramount in his mind at that moment. "I don't know what it is about you," he muttered, sweeping his arm across his desk to clear the surface. Half a dozen file folders and their contents tumbled to the floor in a shower of white and manila. "All the women I've known, and you're the only one who can make me forget everything but this." He tumbled her back onto the desktop, cradling her head with his hands.

She stared up at him, her mouth parted. She tugged impatiently at his shirt. "Have there been many?"

He straightened enough to tear open the buttons, then slid his arm beneath her, pulling her flat against his chest, skin to skin. *Oh, yeah. That's it.* "Many what?"

"Women," she laughed breathlessly.

"Enough," he said truthfully. "Dammit, where is the zipper on these shorts!" They looked like a little skirt from the front, and from the back they'd driven him nuts with the way the pink garment hugged her rear.

She twisted a little, pulling his hand to the fastening, hidden beneath the skirt flap in the front. He loosened his grip on her, a little regretfully, to yank it down, dashing her clothes away.

"What were they like?"

"You're lying naked on my desk and you want to know what my 'other women' were like?"

"Yes," she said primly. Then ruined the effect by sliding her sleek knee slowly along his side.

"To a one, they were tall, stacked, long-haired blondes." He caught her knee, lowered his head and kissed the curve of it. Thoroughly enjoying the broad daylight filling every corner of the house, thoroughly enjoying the fact that they had nearly an hour all to themselves.

Not that the shower they'd taken together in the middle of the night last night had been at all unsatisfactory. Or the other times he'd managed to get her behind a closed door during nap time. Or the—

"Ah-ha. Just like Beth."

"Who?" Garrett mumbled as his mouth moved against her taut thigh.

Darby laughed softly and tugged him over her, fingers fumbling with his straining fly. "Come here. We're wasting valuable time with this infernal chatter of yours."

Three hours later Darby was glad that she'd decided to leave the triplets at Smiling Faces as she took Regan and Reid to the park where the Summer's End Festival was being held. Not that it felt like the end of summer was nearing, considering how hot and humid it was outside. She knew the babies would have been miserable in the heat.

Regan and Reid had already ridden every one of the kiddie rides. Twice, with no regard for the sweltering afternoon. They'd also tossed pennies into glass dishes, bean bags through holes cut into an enormous smiley face and whipped-cream pies at a giggling, red-nosed clown.

Now the snow cones she'd purchased for Regan and Reid were dribbling over the edges of the white paper holders, leaving sticky blue and red stains on their hands, their faces and their clothes. But their smiles were wide and carefree and two pairs of brown eyes gleamed with excitement.

Darby couldn't wait to tell Garrett what a good time he'd missed.

"I wanna go on that!" Regan pointed.

She swallowed a jolt of dismay. "The Ferris wheel?" She hated the Ferris wheel.

"Me, too. Me, too." Reid jumped up and down.

Darby looked around. "How about the boats over there? They look fun, don't they?" And since they were contained in a man-made pool, they didn't rise above the ground more than five feet.

Regan's expression fell. Her eyebrows drew together, but rather than stomping her feet and demanding, she looked up at Darby. "Please?"

Ohh. Darby's shoulders sagged. She looked from Regan and Reid to the Ferris wheel and back again. She just couldn't do it. As much as she didn't want to disappoint them, there was no way on this earth that she could make herself climb into one of those swinging buckets and lift off from the ground. No way.

"I'm sorry, sugar-pie. But I don't think so." She sighed and looked around. "Let's go sit on that bench for a few minutes and decide what to do instead. Okay?"

Regan made a face, but she took Reid's snow-cone-sticky hand in hers and sat. "Regan, I'd take you on the Ferris wheel if I could," she said gently. "But I— I'm afraid of heights. And I can't let you two go on it alone."

"My mommy was 'fraid of being by herself. She yelled at my daddy 'cause she was 'fraid. Are you gonna yell now?"

Darby brushed Regan's hair away from her forehead

and cupped her round cheek. Poor Elise. She and Marc would never be alone now. "No, sugar-pie. I'm not going to yell."

"Perhaps I could be of assistance."

Darby frowned and craned her neck around, looking behind them at the voice.

"Grampy!" Regan squealed and climbed over the back of the bench, dropping her icy treat onto the ground as she launched herself into Caldwell's arms. Reid was only a second behind, and Darby just stared, not knowing quite what to do.

"I'll take them on the Ferris wheel," the mayor offered. If it bothered him that Reid's snow cone was smashed up against his designer polo shirt, he didn't let on.

"Mayor Carson, I really don't—"

"Please."

It didn't look as if the word sat easily on him. But his green-brown eyes were steady on hers, and Regan was nodding enthusiastically.

If Garrett were there, she knew he would flatly refuse. Torn, she chewed the inside of her lip.

"You can sit right there on the bench and watch us the entire time." His lips twisted, and in that moment he looked so much like Garrett that she felt herself softening.

"All right," she agreed reluctantly, and was rewarded by Regan's yippee. "One ride," she added as she took Reid's melting snow cone from him.

She handed their remaining tickets to Caldwell and sat down again to watch. The mayor set the children on their feet and they held both his hands as they walked over to the small line at the wheel. Within minutes they were sitting in one of the buckets and

Darby couldn't help but smile as Regan and Reid waved to her. She waved back.

Up they went on the Ferris wheel. Until they seemed to be tiny dots against the sky. If it were she up there at the peak of the wheel, she would be as panicked as she'd been on that overcrowded elevator at the courthouse.

The wheel began turning again, stopping occasionally. As their bucket lowered, Darby could see the excited expressions on the children's faces. She could also see the completely devoted expression on their grandfather's face.

Sighing a little, she sat back against the bench and watched while the wheel went around and around. Then the children were racing pell-mell toward Darby, chattering a mile a minute.

Caldwell followed more slowly and stopped several feet away from Darby. His eyes lingered on the children, but he seemed to realize that her allowances could only go so far. "Garrett was right when he said I owed you an apology. I was distraught and I was unkind to you. It was uncalled for."

Darby gathered her wits. Caldwell's son hated being his son. And yes, Caldwell had insulted her that day at the courthouse, but what she'd done was so, so much worse. "Losing your daughter has been a terrible tragedy."

"A tragedy," he repeated, his expression pained. "Yes, it was that." He was silent for a moment and the festive sounds of the carnival surrounded them. "I'm fighting Garrett the only way I can," he said suddenly, startling her even more. "I know, given the chance, he will remove them from my life as completely as he's removed himself."

She was totally, utterly, out of her depth. "Mayor Carson, I think Garrett is the one you need to say this to. Not me."

"He's out to ruin the company that has been in my family for generations. He isn't interested in what I say." His smile was thin, his eyes unreadable. "You're his fiancée. I'm sure he's told you what a failure I was as a father."

A group of women dressed in business suits strolled by eating cotton candy. They called out to the mayor with a wave. He waved back, smiling, greeting them all by name. Then he turned back to Darby and his smooth mayoral smile faded. "Fact is, a lot of us failed Garrett, and to my…shame, I let it happen. But he's made a success of himself despite us." There was a touch of pride in his face at that.

Darby shifted on the bench, beyond discomfort with this entire dialogue. "Mayor…" She didn't know what to say to him. And his expression seemed to indicate that he understood.

He crouched down and held out his arms to hug Regan and Reid. Over their heads he looked at Darby. He glanced back at the Ferris wheel. "Thank you."

She managed a smile. Then felt something sad tear inside her when she heard Regan's soft voice.

"I love you, Grampy," the little girl said.

Caldwell's eyes closed. "I love you, too." Then he cleared his throat, straightened to his feet and walked away.

He didn't look back.

After that the children seemed subdued. They didn't protest when Darby suggested they head to the truck. She strapped everyone in and drove carefully to Smiling Faces for the babies and then home in Garrett's new truck. Her poor green car was still sitting at the curb, deader than a doornail. Garrett wanted to have it towed for scrap, but so far she'd refused to let him arrange it.

Before long, she knew she'd need the car again.

But she didn't want to dwell on that depressing thought, and she took the sticky children inside the house.

It was definitely time for baths.

Maybe while she was washing them up, she could wash away the memory of Caldwell's face when he'd walked away from his grandchildren.

"My mother used to make meat loaf like this," Garrett said.

Darby's fork halted midway to her mouth. She contained her surprise that Garrett had voluntarily mentioned his mother. It had seemed to be one of those off-limit topics. "It's the recipe from the box of rolled oats. Probably been printed on it for years."

"Probably." He reached out and pushed Reid's glass away from the edge of the table in a move so automatic that Darby wanted to smile.

"So did you have fun today?" he asked. His words were directed at the children, but his gaze focused on Darby, sending another message entirely.

She felt her cheeks warm, and quickly rose, beginning to clear the dishes as Regan and Reid chattered about the rides. The cotton candy. The snow cones. She'd promised herself that she would tell Garrett about running into the mayor. After dinner. When the children were settled so they wouldn't have to witness the explosion.

She knew she was taking a chance. But so far, neither Regan nor Reid had mentioned their grandfather. It was cowardly, she knew, but their dinner together had been so pleasant that she'd kept putting off the inevitable.

She began loading the dishwasher and turned back to the table only to find Garrett handing her the last remaining stack of plates. She stuck them in the sink to rinse them.

"I had a fun and exciting day, too, today," he murmured over her shoulder and she accidentally squirted the counter with the sprayer.

"How could inking the deal with Nielson Farms be anything less?" She leaned over to put the plates in the dishwasher, and Garrett's arm sneaked around her waist, lifting her right off her feet.

She gasped and wriggled her legs, but he held her high. "Garrett!"

Regan and Reid goggled. Tad and Keely squished their cooked carrots under their fingers, and Bridget's round little face split into an enormous yawn.

It was so wonderful that she fell a little bit more in love with them all. With one in particular.

"Did you or did you not have fun today?" Garrett demanded, mock fierce, against her ear.

She giggled and covered her mouth with her hand, unable to believe such a silly sound had come from her.

"Well?" His eyes crinkled. "I need to know. You know. For future planning and all."

She threw her arms around his shoulders and nodded, giggling some more. "I think going to the carnival should be an everyday affair."

"Are you gonna get babies in your tummy like my mommy?" Regan's voice broke over their silliness.

Darby's mouth parted. She caught Garrett's look. He set her on her feet, and she tugged her shirt firmly about her hips. "Why would you ask that?"

Regan watched her, seeming way too old for a four-year-old. "Daddy kissed Mommy in the kitchen, and she got the babies in her tummy," she said seriously. "Are you?"

Darby shook her head. "No, sweetheart. Not anytime soon." Aside from that first time at Georgie's...and earlier that afternoon in Garrett's den, they'd taken precautions. The last thing they needed was to increase the ratio of children to adults here. Knowing the truth of that, however, didn't keep her from a lingering, torturing vision of having a baby. Garrett's baby.

"How come?" Regan persisted.

Darby stared at Garrett, silently asking for assistance. He shrugged his shoulders. Then, when the doorbell rang, startling them both, he grinned, unashamedly relieved. "Saved by the bell," he murmured, and went to answer the door.

"Because we're not married," Darby answered Regan hurriedly. She started cleaning up the high-chair trays. The children were obviously only interested in playing with their food. "Now, let's get you guys into your pj's and I'll read you a story before bed."

Since Regan and Reid both loved their nighttime stories, they hurried out of the kitchen. Darby quickly wiped up the triplets' hands and faces, then set them on the floor. They crawled like fury for the living room and their favorite toys.

She reached for the dishcloth to wipe down the table and heard Regan's and Reid's delighted squeals. She started to smile, but stopped when she heard Regan's voice.

"Grampy!"

She clenched the wet dishcloth. Knowing she couldn't hide out in the kitchen, she walked out into the living room, taking in the tableau at a glance.

Garrett, standing in the doorway, stiff as a statue.

Caldwell, carrying a large cardboard box under one arm while his free hand tousled Regan's blond curls.

Regan, who chattered happily about riding the Ferris wheel that afternoon with her beloved Grampy.

Garrett cast her one long look. A look totally devoid of amusement. Of laughter. Of trust.

She sighed and reached for Keely before the tot could climb into the fireplace again. So much for putting off the explosion. She should have told him what had occurred that day as soon as he'd walked in the door.

She saw Caldwell look from his son to her and back again. "These are some things of Elise and Marc's that I thought you should have," he said after a tense moment. "The new owners are moving into their house soon." He pushed the box toward Garrett, who didn't make any attempt to take it from the older man.

Darby's stomach tightened. A more stubborn person she'd never met.

Finally Caldwell just set the box on the floor inside the door. "Well. Good night."

"Can Grampy read us our story?"

Garrett shook his head, his eyes flat.

"Please, Uncle Garrett?"

Darby held her breath.

Then Garrett muttered something unprintable and

strode through the living room, into the kitchen and out the back door.

"I guess that's a no," Caldwell murmured, after the screen door slapped shut.

"No," Darby corrected softly. She knew if Garrett had wanted to say no he would have, and that would have been that. He never would have just walked away from the situation. She stared through the kitchen at the closed screen door. "I don't believe that was his answer, at all." And it made her realize, just then, how well she was coming to know this man who'd captured her heart.

Chapter Fifteen

"He's gone?"

Darby didn't need to ask who Garrett meant. She nodded and, since he hadn't frozen her out with a cold look when she'd tentatively stuck her head outside the back door, pushed the screen door wider and walked out onto the porch.

"Is there anything else you did today that you haven't told me about?" He was sitting on the wood-and-wrought-iron bench, one boot propped against the railing opposite him. Even his voice was deceptively smooth. But the rhythmic ticking in his jaw betrayed him.

She shook her head, feeling a bit the way she had the first time she'd told her father that yes, she was still going to nursing school even though he'd promised to cut her off financially if she did. And because she felt that way, her spine stiffened.

"The carnival was in a public park, Garrett. What was I supposed to do? Grab up the children and run screaming for the car as if he's some monster? I'm sorry I didn't tell you right away. All he did was take Regan and Reid on the Ferris wheel, and all three of them loved it."

He didn't answer. His eyes were flat. "I don't want him around them."

Impatience swept through her. "Why not? Garrett, he loves them. Surely even you can see that."

"He's not capable of love. No more than I am."

"Why?" She wrapped her fingers around the metal railing. "Because he never acknowledged you as his son?"

"Because he took my mother's heart and stomped it into the dust," he said unemotionally. "Her family had always worked for the Carsons. When she was sixteen she became a maid there herself. Working before and after school. Even after I was born she stayed on. And after she banished me to New Mexico, she still worked there. And Caldwell, he just…let it continue."

She frowned. It did sound odd to her, but not enough to explain Garrett's deep distrust. "I still don't understand."

"Yeah, well, you don't have to understand," he said flatly. "It's none of your business."

She jerked back. He was right, of course. It wasn't her business. But—

"Wait a minute! You asked me to marry you! Said I would be their…their *mother*. And it is 'none of my business?'"

His eyebrow peaked. "Are you finally accepting my proposal, then?"

"And what? If I say yes, you'll let me in on the big secret about your father, and if I say no, I'll just have to be content with my curiosity?" She stared at him. Loving him. Hating him. Hating herself. Because he'd offered her nearly everything she'd ever wanted in life, and she had no hope of accepting it.

It was probably just as well that he hadn't offered her his heart.

Garrett's jaw was white with tension. "My mother worked there until she got into Caldwell's wife's medicine chest and swallowed too many of her tranquilizers. And Caldwell didn't even trouble himself to attend her funeral. *Now* do you get it?"

She pressed her hand to her heart, horrified. "Oh, Garrett. I'm sorry. I didn't know."

"Nobody knew," he said flatly. "Except Caldwell…and Elise. I came back from New Mexico for the funeral, and Elise couldn't wait to tell me."

"How old were you?"

"Eighteen."

She swallowed and folded her hands together. If only she could hate him. Then when she had to walk away it wouldn't feel so much like dying.

But his mother, it seemed, had been as responsible for Garrett's unhappiness as Caldwell had been, and Darby had to make him see reason about the children. "You're their legal guardian, Garrett. I know the mayor says he wants guardianship himself, but I think it's more knee-jerk than anything. It's not as if he's going to kidnap them or something from you. You can't pretend he's *not* their grandfather just because you pretend he's not your father. The children lost their parents. Don't make them lose the rest of their family, as well."

She watched him. Waited painfully for him to say something. He just sat there like a stone, watching her back. And the last little bit of hope inside her, the wishful kernel that wanted to believe there was some miraculous way that everything could work out, shriveled.

They really didn't know each other at all. Despite everything. And she was even more guilty of that fact than he was.

"You're right," she said stiffly. "It is none of my business. I am only the nanny. The temporary nanny." She turned on her heel and yanked open the screen door.

"Darby."

Just that. Her name. And her feet stopped. She looked at the screen, knowing she should leave before things got even worse, but unable to take... one...more...step. "What?"

"When I told you that Karl had phoned. About Georgie going into the hospital. Do you remember your first thought?"

Her throat tightened and she let the screen door close again.

"Your father," he reminded evenly. "You thought something had happened to your father. Even before thinking of Georgie, regardless of this feud you've got going between you and your family, you thought of your father."

"Your point?" she asked tightly.

Garrett looked at Darby. Explaining didn't come easy for him. But he knew if he didn't, he could write off his chances. With her. With the kids. He might as well give up and let the old man have the fearsome five, because without someone in their lives so filled with loving the way Darby was, his nieces and nephews were no better off with him than they would be with Caldwell.

But he would never give up. Not on this.

So he had to make her understand.

"There must have been some point in your life, growing up, when you knew who you were." She seemed to pale, and he stifled an oath, pushing impatiently to his feet to move down the steps to the grassy yard. He understands a lot more about her than she thought he did, if she would only open up and let him in on her own share of secrets and the past she was running from. "You had a home...with your parents—at least until they divorced. And with your brother. I didn't."

"Lots of people grow up in single-parent families."

"I grew up with a father who acted as if I didn't exist and a mother who put everything aside, including me, in favor of *him.* It didn't matter that the guy was married. Not to him. Not to her. Twisted, if you ask me. I never did know why she even chose to have me, much less keep me."

He smiled grimly. "And then there was Elise. My half sister. Pretty, blond-haired, brown-eyed Elise. She was a year younger than me. We went to the same school. She had everything. Caldwell. Her mom. My mom."

"Garrett—"

"Don't. Don't look at me with pity in your eyes. It was a long time ago, but you might as well understand why things are the way they are."

She sat down on the step, clasping her knees close with her slender arms.

"It wasn't until I was ten that I really started to

grasp it. I was in a lot of sports. Baseball. Soccer. Basketball. Whatever season it was, I was in the after-school program. I liked it. Better to be there than go home to an empty house.''

He closed his eyes for a minute. Remembering that house. It hadn't been a hovel by any means. Caldwell wouldn't have allowed that. It had been comfortable and well furnished, but it had still been empty. Empty because his mother was always at Caldwell's stone mansion.

He dragged his thoughts back in line. ''Anyway, at the end of the baseball season, the coach had a party. Where the trophies are handed out. You know. Most improved player. Stuff like that.''

He shoved his fingers through his hair and laughed grimly. ''It's been a long time since I even thought about this,'' he admitted.

''What happened?''

''All the parents were there. Except mine.''

''You mean Caldwell.''

''I mean my mother,'' he corrected flatly. ''She'd chosen to be at Elise's birthday party, instead. The coach finally gave me a ride home from the pizza place where the party was held when it became apparent that nobody was coming to get me.''

''Oh, Garrett.''

''Elise made sure that everyone at school knew that my own mother preferred to cut cake and wash dishes at her birthday party than to see me get my stupid trophy for most valuable player. I wouldn't even care so much about that except the only fun Elise seemed to get out of it wasn't her birthday party, with the fifty guests and the pony rides and the clowns, but getting to rub my nose in what she had that I didn't.''

Darby rose, silently walking over to him. She folded his hands in hers.

"She was a spoiled brat, and even with the attention of her parents and my mother, she was no happier with her life than I was with mine."

"What happened to Elise's mother?"

He looked at their hands. His looked big and clumsy and brown against her ivory ones. "She went back to England. That's where she was from." His lips twisted. "Came from some rich family over there with titles and God knows what. Elise stayed here in Fisher Falls until Caldwell bought her way into college. As far as I know her mom never divorced Caldwell."

"Then the children *do* have more relatives."

Garrett shook his head. "Hayden did a thorough search. Marc grew up in an orphanage. Elise's mother died several years ago. There's only me. And Caldwell. And I'll be damned if I'll let him do to them what he did to us."

"So you'll ostracize him from the children's lives, instead. Just the way you felt ostracized yourself. When your new office is up and running here in Fisher Falls and the judge gives his final ruling in a few weeks, you'll take them away and never give him an opportunity to see them again." Just as the mayor feared.

"Don't make it sound as if it's some cruel thing. They'll survive. They'll thrive, thanks to you."

Darby looked into his face. "They would thrive, thanks to you, if you let yourself."

"Dammit, Darby, I don't love them. I never will. I don't have it in me. I'll make sure they have everything they need in life, but I can't give them love. I can't give *anybody* that. I wanted them only because I knew it would make the old man crazy.''

He really believed it, and her heart broke for all of them. For the boy he'd been, standing on the outside looking in. For the man he was, hard and driven and unwilling to acknowledge his own needs. "I think you're wrong. I think you're infinitely capable of loving.''

''Why? Because you and I have great sex?''

She flinched at his harsh demand. "Whether you admit it or not, you have a great deal of compassion. Tenderness. And not just in bed with me.''

She swallowed past the gargantuan knot in her throat. "What will you do if the judge doesn't award you permanent custody? It could happen, you know. Or if you do get it, Caldwell could petition for visitation rights. Grandparents have been doing that, and succeeding. What are you going to do then?''

''Then I'll take Caldwell back to court until I *do* win. The only reason I brought G&G to Fisher Falls was because I knew we could put Castle Construction out of business for good. My resources will outlast Caldwell's. And in the end, I *will* win.'' There was no doubt in his expression. "I always do.''

''And the children will grow up being at the center of this war between you and their grandfather, all so that you can sleep at night, knowing you have finally *won* this little—'' she turned away from him, waving her hands impatiently ''—revengefest against your father.''

''They'll live.''

''Like I lived.'' What could she do to make him see the awfulness of his reasoning? "From the time I was nine until I turned thirteen, my parents waged a war against each other for custody of my brother and me. They dragged up every possible, hideous thing they could throw at each other, whether it was true or not.

"And they did it thinking that none of it would affect Dane or me. But they were wrong. Newspapers, friends, television. Everywhere we turned, there it was. The great battle for the—"

Dear God. She'd almost said it. For the Rutherford kids. The heirs to a transportation empire.

"For the what?"

She realized her cheeks were wet. "For the two of us." She turned away from him, wiping away the tears.

The evening had darkened. Crickets chirped to life. The outside light next door flicked on, casting half its glow into Garrett's yard.

"And when you were engaged to the joker, you thought you'd have a life that erased the past."

She didn't deny it. But she'd come to realize that it wasn't losing Bryan that had hurt so badly, but losing the dream of a perfect life where divorce had no place. Where custody battles didn't exist.

"I don't know why Elise said what she did," he admitted. "But maybe she'd realized the same things I had. And she—hell, I don't know—gambled that I was a better bet than our old man. Marry me, Darby." His voice was low. "Come back to New Mexico with me. You'll have the children."

"But none of us will have your love." And she knew she wanted it. With every fiber of her soul, she wanted Garrett's love. She wanted it all. She wanted to know that his nieces and nephews had his love.

Even *want* wasn't the right word.

She *needed* it. For herself. For the children. But

most of all, for him. She looked back at him, waiting for a response.

He said nothing. And that was answer enough.

She was caught so thoroughly in a web of her own making that she honestly didn't know which way to turn.

She couldn't tell him that she didn't want to marry him, because she did. She wanted to make a life with him and the children. She couldn't bear the idea of leaving them.

But she couldn't marry him without telling him the whole truth about herself. And once he knew who she was, he wouldn't want to marry her, anyway. He wouldn't want her anywhere near the children. Because her presence in Fisher Falls had brought more harm to their family than anything Caldwell or Garrett could ever do.

"What are you thinking?"

She folded her arms around herself, chilled. "That no matter what we try to do, life is never cookie-cutter perfect."

"Did you think it would be?"

The ache inside her went too deep for tears. "I kept hoping." And in her search she'd only made things worse.

"I guess that was a lesson I learned a lot younger than you. The only person we can count on is ourselves, and happily ever after exists only in books."

"I don't want to believe that, Garrett." She drew in a long breath. Let it out slowly. "I love you."

"You love everyone. I've seen it. In everyone you meet you find something about them to care about."

"I'm not talking about caring. About one human relating the best way they can to another, which you know very well *you* are more than capable of. For heaven's sake, Garrett. Carmel and Hayden are loyal to you to a fault. Do you think that is only because you pay them for it? It's because of the caring among you.''

He so easily discounted her profession of love, but she wouldn't let it hurt her. Not yet. There would be plenty of time for that.

The rest of her life.

''I'm talking about *love.*'' She stressed the word. ''I love you. Maybe you think that doesn't exist, but I'm telling you that it does.''

''Just because your first time was in that sunroom at Georgie's house with the falls running outside doesn't mean the legend has come true.''

She'd been wrong. The ache wasn't too deep for tears. She looked at him in the half-light, her vision glazed. ''This isn't about a silly legend. It's about what's in my heart. And one day, oh, God, one day I pray that you let someone get past the walls you've built around your heart. That you let yourself love someone back. Because in the end it doesn't matter how perfect the cookie was. How much money you have in the bank, how many houses you've built or how many reporters you've managed to elude. The only thing that matters is love. Love between a parent and a child. Love between a man and a woman.''

''I didn't say that I think love doesn't exist.''

''No,'' she agreed softly as she turned to go back into the house. ''You think you can stand back from it and let other people feel it. But until you step forward, and get right in the muck of all those emotions, it won't matter how tidily you provide a caring parental figure for those children or how much you provide for their physical needs. They'll still grow up looking at you and wondering what they've done wrong that you don't love them back.''

''Daaaarby!''

Garrett sat on the lumpy sofa in the living room and heard soft footsteps overhead. Darby. Going to Reid again. It had been weeks since the boy had wakened like that. He'd actually begun to hope that the restless sleeping episodes might be over. That Darby's steady attention to the kids was having its effect.

Reid was still crying, and Garrett stood up, heading to the stairs. His bare toe painfully jammed the box that Caldwell had left by the door, and he swore under his breath, shoving it out of his way. Damn Caldwell, anyway.

He went up the stairs, stuck his head in the second bedroom. He could see Darby sitting on Reid's bed in the dark, holding him in her lap. He could hear her humming softly. And then he heard something else. Reid humming, too.

He cupped his hand around the doorjamb and stood outside the doorway, looking in.

Where he'd always been.

I love you, she'd said.

Darby could say whatever she wanted. Believe what she needed to believe. But no one had ever loved him before, and he couldn't let himself fall into the trap of thinking that she really did. Because as soon as he did, she'd come to her senses and go back to the life she'd been running from. The life she didn't feel she could fully share with him, despite her pretty words of love.

''Garrett?''

He realized that Darby was looking at him from within the darkness of the room.

His jaw ached. He consciously relaxed. "Yeah. I wanted to make sure Reid was okay."

She stood up from the bed, walked soundlessly toward him. God. She was such a bitty thing.

"He's asleep." She stayed inside the room, leaving a few good feet between them.

"He called your name this time. In his sleep he cried for you."

She made a soft sound. "Yes."

"You're crying," he realized. He reached for her, pulling her out into the hallway. Her robe swished, revealing her bare toes. "Because of Reid?"

"Because of us all." She wiped her cheeks. "I can't do this anymore, Garrett. It's wrong. You don't know—"

"Do what? Go to a crying kid at two in the morning?"

"No. Yes." She pushed her hands through her hair, turning away from him. "All of it."

His gut ached. "Well. That didn't take long. Six, seven hours, to come to your senses." *I love you. What a damn joke.*

"What?"

He pushed his hands into the pockets of his jeans, because if he didn't he was going to do something stupid. Like reach for her and tell her anything so long as she didn't take back her love and go away. It was better that he put the distance between them.

"I'll be gone early in the morning," he told her abruptly. "We're checking out some property in Colorado."

"But it's Satur—"

"We have to move fast on it. If words get out, they'll jack the price up."

"You, um, didn't mention a trip before."

"It didn't come up."

"How long are you going to be gone?"

He shrugged. "Day and a half, maybe."

"I...see," she said faintly. But he knew she didn't.

"Carmel will know how to reach me if you need anything."

"I'm sure we'll be fine."

He nodded, thinking that she should have added *without you.* But even if she'd come to her senses about loving him, it just wasn't in Darby's nature to be so cold.

No matter how true the words would have been.

Chapter Sixteen

"Stubborn...pigheaded man. Can't see beyond the nose on his stubborn, handsome face."

In the weeks since Darby had moved in with Garrett and his crew, she'd gotten into the habit of mopping the tile floors on Saturday mornings. Just because her life was falling apart around her ears didn't mean the floors didn't need a good cleaning.

Now her nose ran and her eyes watered. From the smell of the floor cleaner she'd dumped into the water, she assured herself. That's the only thing it could be, because she was tired of crying over that big... dumb...man.

"I see he's got you swabbing the decks now."

She nearly jumped out of her skin at the voice behind her and turned to see Hayden Southerland outside the front screen door. Her in-the-cellar stomach took an even deeper nosedive.

She stuck the mop in the bucket and moved to the door, flipping loose the latch. "Hayden. I figured you would be with Garrett."

"He's not here?"

"No." Twenty floors underground. That's where her stomach was now. "He went to Colorado," she said, feeling awkward. Stupid. She knew that Garrett unfailingly included Hayden in his business plans. "He said he was looking at a property there."

"Right. Of course." Hayden was nothing if not smooth. He tapped the manila envelope he held against his palm. "I didn't really need him, anyway. I can give these to you just as easily." He handed her the envelope.

"What is it?"

"The prenup. You guys just read it through, make sure everything is covered the way you want, and if it is, sign whenever you like." He smiled faintly. "As long as it's before the wedding. Speaking of which, have you set a date yet?"

"Ah, no. No. Not yet." She stared at the envelope.

"It'll be a big event when you do."

"Why?"

He laughed. "Because as long as I've known Garrett, he's been anti-marriage. Guess it took a petite redhead to change his mind after all those tall blondes."

Not exactly. What it had taken was five orphaned children. She was only a by-product, as far as Garrett was concerned. "I'll pass these on to Garrett." She made herself smile casually. "Thanks for bringing them by."

"Sure." He started to leave, but paused. "You

know, I still can't help thinking we've met before. Where did you say you came from?"

She hadn't. Which he knew perfectly well. But he was Garrett's attorney and his friend, and she couldn't blame the man for being naturally curious. "I think I'd remember meeting a man like you." Her smile was polished, her delivery smooth. And as insincere as anything she'd said in weeks. Months.

The corner of his lips lifted, and she knew he hadn't been fooled for a second. "Well. Have Garrett give me a call when you see him."

"Will do." She kept her smile in place until Hayden climbed in his low-slung black car and roared off down the street. Then she latched the screen door again and slapped the envelope down on Caldwell's cardboard box that she'd stuck on the stairs so it wouldn't get wet when she mopped the foyer. But when she did, she knocked the box off the edge and it tumbled on its side, dumping the contents out onto the damp floor.

"Oh, sure. Make more of a mess." She crouched down and righted the box, reaching for the items that had fallen from it. Several children's books. A blanket. A jewelry box.

She shifted until she was sitting on a step and flipped open the small pink-and-white box. The little ballerina inside spun, the music tinkling merrily.

"What's that?"

Darby looked up and drew Regan next to her. She touched the strands of brightly colored beads inside the box. "These were your mother's," she told Regan gently. "Your grandpa brought them over for you to have."

The little girl chewed her lip for a minute, then

stuck her fingers where Darby's had been. She drew out a pink-and-white beaded necklace. "Can I wear it?"

"Yes." Darby undid the little clasp and fastened it around Regan's neck.

"Am I pretty as my mommy?"

Darby smiled shakily. She started to speak, but someone beat her to it.

"Prettier," Garrett said from the doorway. He pulled open the screen and stepped inside the house.

Darby could only stare at him. "Fast trip to Colorado."

"Plans changed." His smile wasn't much of one, but it wasn't a snarl, either. And when he looked at Regan, preening with her pretty, little-girl necklace, his expression gentled. "What have you got there?"

She took the jewelry box from Darby's numb fingers and held it up. "See? Do I get to keep it all?"

"Looks like."

Regan whooped. She started to run back to the kitchen, but turned around and trotted back. "Does Reid and the babies got any presents, too?"

Garrett looked at the tumbled things on the floor. "I don't know. Probably. Let's look."

Darby scooted up a few steps, quickly giving Garrett a place to sit, drawing her legs close. Then she watched as Garrett, Mr. I'll-provide-for-them-but-never-love-them reached for the books she'd already put back in the box.

He held them out for Regan. "More bedtime stories for you guys."

Regan plopped down on the tile and set the books in her lap. "What else?" Her eyes danced. She reached for a thick album lying facedown, and Garrett helped her pick it up.

"It's a scrapbook." He flipped through several pages. "Report cards from school. Some old pictures and stuff. Look. That was your mommy when she was just a little older than you."

Darby looked over Garrett's shoulder to see him pointing at a school class picture.

Regan peered. "She was little."

"Yes, she was," Garrett murmured.

"Was you bestest friends with her like me 'n Reid?"

Darby saw Garrett's shoulders go still. "Not quite like you and Reid," he said after a moment. "Look. This must've been her baby blanket." He plucked the soft-blue receiving blanket out of the box and flicked it open over Regan's crossed legs, making her giggle.

"What's this?" Regan pointed to the corner.

"Initials. Should be your mo—"

Darby sat forward when Garrett's words cut off. "G. C. C." she read softly.

Garrett suddenly stood. He grabbed up the manila envelope that had his name printed on the outside. "What's this?"

"Papers from your lawyer."

"Uncle Garrett, can I give the blankie to the babies?"

"Yeah. Sure."

Regan popped to her feet and skipped into the kitchen bearing her assortment of treasures.

"That was your blanket, wasn't it," Darby murmured. "Garrett C. Cullum. *C* for what? Caldwell?"

"Carson." He bit out the word.

She nodded, chewing her lip for a moment. "Saved all these years."

"It's just a blanket," he said tightly. "Stuck in a box with a bunch of other old junk that doesn't matter to anybody but a bunch of little kids."

"It looked handmade to me," she observed mildly.

"So?"

"So-o-o nothing. Just seems kind of interesting that it's in the stuff from Caldwell. Maybe he wasn't as oblivious to you as you thought." She didn't wait for a reply to that, but jerked her chin toward the sturdy envelope that he'd crumpled in his grip as she stood, also.

"Your attorney is a little behind the times." Her voice was smooth. "He seems to think you and I are getting married."

She descended the few steps and bent down to pick up the rest of the books that had fallen from the box. They weren't children's books, though. They were three lined journals filled by a slanting feminine hand. She held them out to Garrett. "Looks like Elise kept a diary."

He eyed them as if they were serpents. "I don't want 'em."

"Well, your...the mayor must have had some reason for sticking them in here. Maybe Elise wrote about the children or something." She pushed the slender tomes into his free hand. "Maybe you'll find some understanding of her."

"I don't want to read her damned journals."

"Afraid of what you might find?" She regretted the words as soon as she said them. "Oh, Garrett. Whether you read them or not is up to you. But you can't throw them away. The children might want them someday."

"Fine." His tone was clipped. "I won't throw them out."

She considered that quite a concession. She quickly tipped the last few items—an old pocket watch with the engraved name Northrop nearly worn away; a leather folder containing Elise's and Marc's diplomas; a padded case—back into the box and started to fit the lid back on.

"What was in that last case there?"

She removed it again and handed it to Garrett. "I don't know. I didn't look." She took the box and set it inside the door to Garrett's den. When she returned, he was looking at the opened case.

Leaving him to it, she plucked the mop out of the bucket, wrung it out and dashed it over the faint footprints she and Regan had left with their bare feet.

"I thought I made it clear that I didn't expect you to do that sort of thing."

"Who do you think has been keeping the house clean all this time? Fairies?"

"There are cleaning services."

"Maybe I like taking care of a house," she said bluntly.

He laughed shortly. "Come on, Darby. What woman wouldn't want to give up mopping and dusting given the opportunity? Except my mother."

Darby ignored that last bit that he'd tacked on with grim sarcasm and focused on the first part. "One who was never given an opportunity to do it before!" She slammed the mop back into the bucket, making the water slosh. She didn't know where the sudden anger came from. But it was just there.

"You like cleaning a house," he said slowly. Skeptically.

She propped her hands on her hips and looked at him. So strong and intense and capable. So stubborn and deliberately alone, even when he was surrounded by people wanting to love him.

Yes, she did know where her anger came from, and there wasn't one darned thing she could do to correct the situation.

"I like taking care of a home," she corrected tightly. And not just any home, she knew. *His* home. Children or not. "I like feeling needed, and yes, that's something new to me, too."

Her eyes drifted from his face to the padded case in his hand. All the frustration and anger inside her dissolved, leaving her feeling drained. "Those are wedding rings." Two gold bands, one wide and plain, the other studded with a trio of enormous diamonds. "Elise and Marc's."

"Yeah. I remember Elise flashing the thing when we ran into each other at the deli."

Her chest was tight. "I have to tell you something," she whispered.

He squeezed the case shut. "Don't bother. I already know what you're gonna say."

Her lips moved, but no words emerged. Then her throat unlocked enough for a croak. "You...know."

"You don't want to marry me. You don't want to watch the kids anymore. You want to forget about the love you claimed to have for us all, keep on moving, never getting involved, never trusting anything or anybody long enough to even open a goddamned checking account."

She swayed. "You're the one who doesn't get involved."

"I'm involved up to my eyeballs," he said savagely. "I couldn't even get on the flight to Colorado this morning because of you and the kids. Because I didn't want to come back and find that Caldwell had gotten to you, or because you'd decided to cut your losses and run."

"Run?"

"Like you were doing when you came to Fisher Falls. What'd your father do? Beat you?"

She frowned. "Beat? No! No he didn't beat me. You say you were ignored by your parents. Well, I was suffocated by mine. I met only those whom they wanted me to meet. My friends were chosen for me. My...my *life* was mapped out, planned out, bought and paid for."

Even thinking about her life before she'd escaped made her feel panicky and trapped. She moved past him to the screen door, pushing it open. Where she could feel the morning sun on her face. Where she could breathe the green, open space.

"Even after their divorce and my mother moved away to New York," she whispered, "it was the same whether I was at home or with her. Drivers who had bulges under their jackets because of the weapons they carried. Security systems on the houses. The cars. Bodyguards I wasn't supposed to know about, but I *did*, following me everywhere I went. Finishing school. Nursing school."

She pressed her hands to her eyes, trying in vain to block out the memories. "Do you know what it's like, Garrett, to have every move you make documented by somebody? By the people who are supposed to be protecting you from harm? By the reporters who want a photo of the poor little rich girl? By the...men who think if they smile pretty enough at you they can convince you you're the love of their life when all they want is a chance at Daddy's millions?''

''Is that what happened with Bryan?''

''No. Bryan Augustine was actually *offered* millions to make me his wife. Only I didn't find out about that until after he'd decided on our wedding day that I wasn't worth the money after all, because he wanted to reconcile with his ex-wife.''

Her eyes burned. ''All I wanted was to be left alone. To live my life outside of a fishbowl for once, outside of my father's world. I wanted to walk down the street and have someone smile at me just because. I thought I'd been careful enough. I changed my looks. I gave up nursing and lived on what I earned at Smiling Faces. I didn't sign any leases, didn't get any parking tickets, didn't even get a library card, renew my driver's license or join a church.''

Her voice was hoarse. ''I never meant for anything bad to happen, Garrett. You have to believe me. I'd take it all back if I could. I'd go home and never try to escape again if only I could.''

Tears streamed down her cheeks. ''But I can't. I can't take back my love for you. I can't bring back Elise and Marc.''

''Nobody's asking you to.''

''That's because you don't know the truth. It's my fault. All of it.''

''What is?''

''The accident,'' she whispered. ''Phil Candela was looking for me. He was my father's head of security.''

''At Rutherford Transportation,'' he murmured. ''They're into everything. Shipping. Airlines. Trucking.''

''Rail, oil, manufacturing,'' she added tiredly. She

could have gone on. But what was the point? Rutherford Transportation said it all. She drew in a long breath, let it out slowly, wondering why it felt like such a relief to admit it, knowing that it signaled the end of her dreams.

"I didn't mean to love you, Garrett. I'm sorry. I tried so hard not to."

"Darby—"

"My real name is Debra White Rutherford. Darby's the nickname my brother gave me when I was little. And if Phil Candela hadn't been searching for me on behalf of my father, your sister and her husband would still be alive. And so would Phil."

Feeling curiously calm, she walked down the three steps of his front porch.

Garrett handled multimillion-dollar deals every week, but he didn't have one damned clue how to handle this.

Darby was walking across the lawn, her bare feet sinking into the neatly groomed grass. He hadn't mowed it. Which meant that she probably had.

Another thing she'd grown up never having to do.

He strode across the lawn and caught her arms. "Where do you think you're going?"

She shrugged, her eyes glazed. "What does it matter? You can't want me to stay here."

He stifled an oath and steered her off the sidewalk and back onto the grass. "You don't even have on shoes," he muttered.

She strained against him. "Garrett, please. I can't bear this."

"Tough. I'm not letting you go." He pulled her back inside the house, into the den. The kids were still occupied, thankfully. "I saw the magazine, Darby. The one you keep in the drawer upstairs."

She jerked. Went still.

"When Georgie first went into the hospital, before her surgery. I put away some laundry and some of your things were in the load with the kids' stuff. When I put them away in the drawer, I saw the magazine." He grimaced, remembering the jolt it had caused him to see Darby's face staring at him from the glossy pages. Every single unusual thing he'd ever noticed about her had suddenly made so much sense. "I've known who you really were ever since."

She sank down onto the sofa. "And I was worried that Hayden had recognized me, but you've known for days. Why didn't you say something?" she whispered.

"Why didn't you?" He sighed roughly. "Because you've been blaming yourself for the accident," he answered his own question. "Dammit, Darby. It was pretty apparent that you were hiding from something. When I saw the magazine, well, I didn't know what to think, to be honest. It's hard for me to picture you as that...American princess."

"I'm not."

"That's how every article ever printed about you refers to you. But you know how to bake meat loaf, for God's sake."

"I learned how to cook from a woman I met in college," she said dully. "Susan thought it was hilarious that I didn't know how to boil an egg. My father's housekeeper, Marlene, was scandalized every time I ever tried to even enter the kitchen." Her lips twisted. "The only reason Susan was in the same classes as I was, that she...befriended me...was because my father had paid her to be there. I thought she was an older woman who'd decided to go back to college and get a degree. But she was only a bodyguard.''

"Bodyguards don't get paid to help another person learn how to cook. Maybe she really did like being your friend. Did that occur to you?''

"After I graduated I never saw her again. That's what I know,'' Darby said flatly.

"Well, I don't know your father, and he doesn't know me. I'd hoped that you'd tell me, someday, about yourself. But it didn't change anything. Not for me. Heiress or not, you are still the woman who cares the most about my kids.''

Her hands were trembling and he sat down beside her, pulling her toward him. "If I'd known you were blaming yourself for the car accident—ah, Darby. It was an *accident*. Don't make it worse by walking away now!''

Darby was trembling so badly she could feel her teeth chattering. "I can't stay. Surely you can understand—''

He gave her a hard, searing kiss, silencing her. "I understand that,'' he said evenly. "I understand that those kids in the other room need a mother, and dammit, Darby, you *know* you're the best woman for the job.''

"You still want me to marry you?''

"I haven't heard anything to make me change my mind,'' he said flatly.

"But my family—''

"Could buy and sell me a hundred times over.''

"Nobody could buy you. But word would get out.''

"So? Let it.''

"Garrett, you don't know what it's like. If it's not my father thinking he can engineer everyone's lives to suit his purposes, then it's the reporters who regularly camp out, outside my family's home, waiting for a shot of us coming and going. Some don't even wait. They climb fences and disable security cameras in order to get a closer view.''

''Is that why you came to Fisher Falls? To get away from the media attention?''

''To get away from that. To get away from my father. He's…impossible, Garrett. He refuses to believe that I am able to live my own life safely.'' She pressed her fingertips to her throat. ''Honestly, Garrett, his worrying over me wasn't healthy for any of us.''

''Because of the kidnapping.''

Darby looked away. ''You really do know.''

Garrett sighed. ''I remember when it happened. It was big news, Darby.'' She'd been only eight or nine. Little. Stolen right out in plain sight, in the confusion of a crowded elevator. The entire country had been outraged. The president himself had promised retribution. And when she'd been found, days later, gagged and bound on the roof of some abandoned warehouse, her photo had been on every magazine and newspaper in the country.

''The kidnapping wasn't even for the ransom,'' Darby said. ''It was a reporter who did it. Alan Michaels. He'd thought he would make a name for himself when he 'rescued' me.''

''He was insane.''

''Michaels has been institutionalized ever since, but Daddy still considers him a threat to me. He blamed my mother for not keeping me in better sight. It was the start of the end of their marriage.''

''And your father has tried to keep you in a protective, gilded cage ever since.''

"I didn't want to hurt him, Garrett. But when he made the administrator at the Schute Clinic fire me, I couldn't take it another second."

"Why did he do it? The administrator, I mean."

She shook her head. "I don't know. Not even Georgie, who supports the clinic with enormous bequests, could sway the clinic administrator. And then one of the local papers got word that I'd been dismissed, and speculation took off—everything from having an affair with the sixty-year-old married administrator to stealing drugs from the pharmacy. I couldn't take it anymore. I had to get away."

"Why didn't you correct them? Issue your own statement or something. Hell, you could hire a public relations firm to put out fires like that for you."

"And just have more people telling me what to wear, where to dine, whom to associate with, what to say in public? No, thanks. And what would I say in a statement, anyway? My father had me fired because I finally wanted to move away from home?" She hopped to her feet and paced. "Nobody would believe me. I mean, who lives that way? It's ridiculous! I'm ridiculous!"

"I believe you," he said evenly. "I don't find you ridiculous. I don't give one good damn who your family is. You've proven that you can make a life on your own without them, whether you recognize that fact or not. I still think you should marry me."

"Haven't you listened to anything I've said?"

"Have *you* listened to what I've said? The accident wasn't your fault any more than it was mine. You love my kids and they love you. What else is there to care about?"

"The future," she said huskily. "Love. Even if I

thought the day might come when I could hold those children in my arms and *not* feel guilty about the loss of their parents, I can't marry you just to provide a mother for them. I can't stand by and watch you close them off from their grandfather and just keep my mouth shut about it because you disagree. I can't do any of that.''

''So what are you going to do,'' he asked flatly. ''Run away again?''

She flinched. ''I told you that I'd help you with the children until you were finished with your business here in town. Unless you are...firing me, that's what I intend to do.''

His dark-green gaze bored into her. ''All right, then, Darby. You're fired.''

Chapter Seventeen

Darby stared at Garrett, shock sweeping through her. On top of everything else, it was just too much. "All right. Fine." She pushed out the words, then turned and ran past the mop and bucket, up the stairs and into the master bedroom.

She slammed the door shut and stood there, shaking like a leaf. He'd fired her.

After all they'd been through, he'd fired her!

She yanked open the drawers beside the bed and shoveled the clothes up in her hands, pushing them haphazardly into the overnighter that she dragged out from beneath the bed where she'd stored it. She opened the minuscule closet and pulled out the red dress she'd worn that unforgettable day and balled it up, adding it to the mess in the soft-sided bag. Shoes. Toiletries. Everything went into the bag with no regard for neatness, no regard for anything but getting the job done as quickly as possible.

She turned back to the small dresser and stared into the drawer at the folded-open magazine. It was the only item left inside the drawer.

She snatched it up, looking at the engagement photo of her and Bryan. For the life of her, she couldn't remember what it was that had attracted her to him. He'd been easygoing, true. And they'd had some fun times together.

But he was nothing like Garrett.

Nobody was like Garrett.

Her eyes burned, and she took the magazine into the bathroom and deliberately dropped it into the small trash container sitting on the floor beside the sink.

Then she shoved her bare feet into her tennis shoes and picked up her bulging overnighter. Going back downstairs took nearly every bit of strength she possessed. Walking past Garrett, who was standing by the couch, his eyes unreadable, took another chunk.

Kissing the children goodbye and not breaking down sapped the rest of her strength.

She turned and went to the entry, staring through the screen door. Her car. It was still sitting at the curb, it's engine deader than a doornail.

Well, she'd walked before, she would walk again.

"You're really going to leave. Just like that. Walk away." Garrett said, coming up behind her.

She stiffened and pushed open the screen. "What's the difference?" She asked painfully. She couldn't look back at Garrett. Not if she wanted to keep from collapsing at his feet and begging for a little more time. "I can do it now, or you can do it in a few weeks after the custody hearing when you'll be free to go back to your home in New Mexico. Either way this ends the same.''

She stepped down the three steps, feeling older than her years, and walked away. Past the Suburban that he'd bought brand-new so he'd have a reliable way to transport his fearsome five. Past the second truck he'd bought so she would have something reliable, too.

She headed down the street, moving blindly.

She knew she'd go to the gatehouse. But it no longer seemed the haven it had once been. And running again didn't seem like the answer it had been four months earlier.

Tears blinding her, she reached the corner and started to cross the street, jumping back at the sharp toot of a horn.

She stood there, shaking, aware of a car stopping right there in the middle of the street where she'd nearly walked right under its wheels, and the driver getting out.

''Darby?''

She focused with an effort. ''Mayor Carson,'' she whispered. ''What are you doing here?''

His eyebrows drew together. ''You're crying.''

She brushed her hands across her cheeks.

''Where are you going?'' He slid the strap of her suitcase off her shoulder and pushed a clean handkerchief into her hands.

Kindness from Caldwell Carson was the last thing she deserved. She shook her head, unable to speak.

He sighed faintly, then took her arm and pushed her into the front seat of his stately sedan. He rounded the car and climbed behind the wheel. ''What's Garrett done now?''

She wiped her eyes. "Nothing. All he's done is love your grandchildren!"

"I know."

"Then why are you trying to take them from him?"

"Why are you walking away from that dinky little house he's rented with a suitcase and tears running down your face?"

"Because I love him and...and it's impossible."

"Love seems to be that way," Caldwell murmured. "Where can I take you?"

"My great-aunt's house. Georgina Vansant's."

Caldwell looked at her. "Georgina is your great-aunt?"

Darby nodded. She looked down the street as the mayor drove away. She watched until her poor green car and Garrett's tidy little house was no longer in sight.

"Roth Rutherford is my father," she admitted dully.

The car jerked a little. "What?"

"I'm Roth Rutherford's daughter, which means you probably also realize that your daughter's accident was my fault," Darby whispered.

"What are you talking about?"

"The other driver was in town because of me. Phil Candela. Because he was looking for me. If I hadn't been hiding out in Fisher Falls from my family, none of this would ever have occurred."

At that Caldwell swerved to the curb and practically stood on the brakes. Darby pitched forward, nearly hitting her head on the dashboard.

Caldwell's arm caught her shoulders and pushed her back against the seat. "You think *you* had something to do with Elise and Marc's accident?"

"I'm so sorry. All I've done by coming to Fisher

Falls is hurt people. I never meant any of it to happen.''

Caldwell suddenly took off again, his foot heavy on the gas as he drove rapidly through town. Darby twisted her hands together. "Mayor Carson, I—"

"Call me Caldwell, Darby. You're going to be my daughter-in-law, after all."

She frowned and stared at him. "I'm not marrying your son. Surely you can understand how wrong it would be."

"It would be the only right thing in this whole damned mess," he said shortly.

"I don't understand."

His lips tightened. "You will." He turned up the drive next to Georgie's and parked in front of the entrance to an ornate, stone mansion. He climbed out of the car, came around and opened her door, waiting.

A jolt of nervousness penetrated the ache inside her. "Why are we here?"

"To get some things straightened out," he said heavily.

She climbed out of the car warily. Accompanied him through the heavy door and along a cool, shadowy corridor where their footsteps echoed hollowly.

Caldwell turned into a spacious study. The walls that weren't lined with stuffed bookcases were filled with framed photographs. He went to the telephone on the desk and picked it up, dialing quickly. Then he gestured toward the red leather chairs in front of his massive desk, but Darby avoided them. She looked around, thinking that Caldwell's study was very much like her father's, only on a smaller scale. She glanced at the photographs hanging on the wall, stopping over a collection of a teenager wearing a baseball uniform.

It was so obviously Garrett when he'd been young.

She started when she heard Caldwell speak Garrett's name into the phone and turned around to look at him. His phone conversation was short. He dropped the phone back in its cradle. "Garrett is on his way."

Garrett sat in his truck and stared at the lines of the stone mansion sitting on the hill.

Caldwell's mansion.

Coming here had been about as appealing as drinking mud, but when Caldwell had said that Darby was there, he'd known he had no choice.

He blew out a harsh breath and climbed out of the truck, striding up the wide steps to the massive front door. He pushed his finger relentlessly against the buzzer.

He didn't know what Darby was doing here, but he'd collect her and they'd get the hell out of there.

After a long moment the door swung open and Garrett's father stood there. Caldwell looked behind Garrett, as if expecting to see more.

"You didn't think I'd bring the children, did you?" The children were safe and sound at home with Carmel at the helm.

"I'd hoped," Caldwell said stiffly as he pushed the door wider. "But it's probably just as well. At least until we get some things resolved."

"Only thing I want resolved is getting Darby out of here. What did you do, snatch her off the street?"

"Garrett."

He looked past Caldwell to see Darby standing there. He brushed past the older man and closed his hands over her shoulders. "Are you all right?"

"I'm fine."

"What are you doing here?"

"Come into my study," Caldwell said. "And I'll try to explain."

Garrett met Darby's eyes. "Let's just get outta here."

"I think you should stay. Hear him out," she said softly. She held up her hand, and Garrett realized she was holding a framed snapshot. "Look."

He took it from her, and his jaw tightened as he recognized himself.

"There are dozens just like this in his study," she murmured. "Please, Garrett. At least listen to what he has to say. He's making an effort. Can't you?"

He grimaced. "Fine." He wrapped his hand around hers and pulled her along with him as he followed Caldwell into the study. Caldwell started to move behind the wide slab of a desk, but changed direction and sat instead in one of the red leather side chairs situated in the corner of the room.

Garrett looked at the other chairs. He didn't sit.

"You haven't read your sister's diaries," Caldwell said.

"I'm not interested in what she had to say," Garrett said flatly. "What does that have to do with anything?"

"If you'd read them, you would have realized that Elise and Marc were getting a divorce."

Garrett stilled. Darby made a distressed sound.

"She and Marc had been having trouble for years. She wasn't what you would call a...devoted mother." Caldwell looked at Darby. "I have never seen the children as happy as they've been in the weeks since you've been caring for them with Garrett."

Darby's hand tightened around Garrett's.

"I made a lot of mistakes as a father," Caldwell continued. "But I've been a good grandfather. The children have spent a lot of time here with me. Elise...she left them here a great deal. I honestly thought that they belonged with me, Garrett. Until I saw for myself how devoted Darby is to them. When I took them on the Ferris wheel, all Regan and Reid talked about was their uncle Garrett and Darby. They were happy. Finally."

Darby sank into one of the chairs. "I don't understand. Elise and Marc seemed devoted to the children."

"Marc was," Caldwell agreed sadly. "Elise...was troubled. She wasn't delighted when she learned she was pregnant again. And when it turned out to be triplets, she was even more unhappy."

"But she didn't even use Smiling Faces full-time for the children."

"No, she didn't," Caldwell agreed. "Because of the way it would 'look' to her friends. She left them here. Fortunately, I have enough household staff that, even if I wasn't here, the children were safe and cared for. I'd agreed to pay for a live-in nanny for them, but Marc flatly refused what he considered more charity from me. Marc had finally had enough of Elise's irresponsible ways. A few weeks before the accident happened, he'd filed for divorce and for custody of the children. Elise was my daughter, but I believed that Marc was doing the right thing. She was livid with me when I told her so."

"So what's that got to do with us," Garrett asked bluntly. "Elise was angry with you because you supported Marc on the divorce, so she was trying to get back at you by saying she wanted me to raise her kids?''

"Garrett," Darby shook her head, her expression pained. "You don't know how badly off she was. I honestly don't think she was in any condition to be scheming."

"We'll never know," Caldwell said. "She was extremely angry with me, but she was angry with Garrett, as well."

"She hated me," Garrett said flatly. "She always did."

"She was jealous of you," Caldwell corrected. "She wanted me to change my will. But she had no need of inheriting any interest in Castle Construction. She had already inherited a fortune from her mother."

"Yet she and her husband lived in a house that you owned."

"Your sister wasn't very prudent where money was concerned. Marc was on the verge of bankruptcy because of her lavish spending habits. She'd have sold off Castle Construction for a quick buck without a second thought." Caldwell's gaze rested on Garrett. "The company is your inheritance, Garrett. I wrote it in my will when you were born. I never intended for that to change. Elise, unfortunately, didn't believe that I'd hold to that decision."

Garrett kept a tight rein on the emotion rampaging inside him. "I don't want it."

"Then you can sell it off. You can absorb it into G&G. You can do whatever you want, once I'm gone. It'll be your right. If it makes you feel better to think about doing that, then go ahead. I don't expect you to feel any sentimental attachment to Castle Construction even though it is part of your heritage. I was a rotten father to you, Garrett.''

''So why were you?'' The words came out without Garrett's permission. His hands curled. ''Never mind,'' he said curtly. ''I don't care anymore.''

Caldwell winced. ''I'm sure you don't. But there were reasons, Garrett. Reasons you knew nothing about.''

''Well maybe you'd better tell me them once and for all.''

''Will you believe what I tell you?''

Garrett's jaw tightened even more. ''I don't know,'' he said truthfully. ''But I'll be damned if I'll let your past screw up my future...or those kids' futures.''

''Then you might as well sit down,'' Caldwell said wearily. ''Because it's a long story.''

Darby chewed her lip. She wanted to go to Garrett and put her arms around him. She wanted to kiss away the deep frown marring his beautiful face.

But she couldn't. It was good that Garrett and his father were trying to resolve their differences. But they didn't need her sitting in the middle of it. ''I should go.''

''No.'' Garrett's hand closed over her shoulder, keeping her in place.

''Garrett, this is between you and Caldwell.''

''He's right,'' Caldwell said. ''You should stay. It concerns you, too. I will drop my suit contesting Garrett's custody of the children as long as I know that the two of you will be together when you raise my grandchildren.''

Darby exhaled shakily. ''I can't marry Garrett just to provide a new mother for the children.''

''Why?'' Garrett asked.

She rose to her feet and stared at him. "Garrett, we've already been through this! You and Elise and Caldwell are perfect examples that secrets can't be kept for good. They fester and they hurt. One day they'll learn that I was responsible for the accident that took their real mother."

"You weren't responsible for the accident, Darby," Caldwell said.

"Why? Because I wasn't driving one of the cars? Phil Candela had no reason to be in Fisher Falls unless he'd discovered a lead on *me*."

"But the fault wasn't his," Caldwell countered gently.

"What?"

He sighed. "As mayor, I have some influence with the police department. I didn't have them change the facts in the police report or anything, but I was able to keep them from issuing the full details of the accident in any statements. There was only one person responsible for the accident, Darby. And that person was my daughter."

"Elise?"

"She was driving. Speeding. No attempt to stop at the red light. Candela was lawfully in the intersection, and she hit him. His car was the only one there. If she hadn't hit him, she'd have driven right through the windows of Smiling Faces. The police determined that there would have been no way for her to stop in time. I couldn't see it serving any good purpose for that information to get out, so I had everyone put a lid on it. Had I known you were blaming yourself, I could have cleared it up weeks ago."

Darby swayed, and Garrett caught her against him. "If you want to focus on the fact that Candela was there, at that moment, at that time, because of you, then you should realize that his presence in that car probably saved a lot of children inside Smiling Faces.''

Darby's eyes filled. ''Molly's had been at capacity for months,'' she admitted. ''And I was standing right there, right in front of the windows. We were playing London Bridge and we heard the crash. Right there.''

''Then he saved you, too,'' Garrett murmured against her temple.

''Just as my father would have expected from the head of his security.'' She wiped her cheeks, looking up at Garrett. ''I should have told you who I was, right from the first. I know that.''

''You didn't because I wielded the kids' welfare over you. I knew you had a price. And I could see in your eyes that it was believing the children needed you. I took full advantage of you. You're a woman full of love and compassion, and I haven't done anything to deserve you. But I still want you to marry me.''

She frowned and glanced at Caldwell who was watching them. ''No. I'm sorry, but I...I can't. I simply can't.'' Then, because she couldn't bear the fierce frowns on the faces of the two men, she hurried out of the room.

Chapter Eighteen

Garrett paused on the hillside and watched Darby staring out at the waterfall. The wind was picking up again, blowing her feathery hair about her head and making the skirt of her sundress flatten against her legs.

He figured they would have another thunderstorm that night. As far as he was concerned the night could split apart with thunder. It suited his mood just fine. He didn't know if he believed all that Caldwell had said after Darby left the room. But he supposed it was as easy to believe as to not.

He strode across the grassy hill toward her. "How many times are you gonna walk away from me?"

She whirled around, her face pale.

"I hope you don't plan to do it a lot, because I gotta tell you, sweetheart, it's not my favorite view of you.

Even if you do have a world-class rear end. Running is just not an option for you anymore.''

"I wasn't running anywhere. You fired me, remember?"

"I fired you because I wanted to shake some sense into you! I wanted you to get mad. To get your back up. To realize that you are *not* incapable of running your own life, of making decisions, of being exactly the person you are!" He breathed roughly and lowered his voice. "I fired you so we could have a fresh start. I wasn't going to let you out of my sight for long. I had no way of knowing that you'd run into Caldwell before we could get things settled between us."

Darby wrapped her arms around herself. She wanted, so badly, to lean her head against Garrett's hard shoulder. But if she weakened now, she'd never find any strength again. "It's hard to take in. What Caldwell said. Elise seemed so devoted to her children."

"That whole family has always been expert at not being what they seemed. Caldwell married his English wife because of the money she brought to their union that would save Castle Construction from ruin thanks to *his* father, but he didn't love her."

"Georgie said he'd sacrificed his own happiness," Darby murmured.

"Then there was my mother," he continued evenly. "Working around his house, being sweet and understanding and everything that his unloving wife wasn't."

His lips twisted. "I was the result of *that*. But if he acknowledged me, his wife would've pulled her money back out of Castle Construction, and the entire town would've suffered because of the loss of jobs.

Caldwell wouldn't fire my mother from his staff, though, even though his wife was livid about it all, because my mother threatened to disappear with me for good. He says he never slept with her again. And the next year, Elise was born.''

''You believe him?''

He looked back over his shoulder at the stone house. ''Who the hell knows. It makes as much sense as anything I've ever come up with. She wasn't a prisoner in Caldwell's house. His wife had to hate her being there. My mom could have left anytime she wanted. She never did.''

''But she did end up sending you away from Fisher Falls. To New Mexico.''

''Probably the smartest thing she did. Not that I thought so at the time. But it got me out of the...weirdness here. Caldwell says he was glad by then, too. He knew my mother wasn't...stable. And then here I've been, prepared to take his grandchildren away, too, where he'd never have access to them again.''

''Oh, Garrett.'' Forgetting everything but him, and the confused, angry boy he must have been, she pressed her hands around his.

''It sort of makes sense,'' he said. ''My mother was obsessed with him. When Caldwell's wife left and went back to England, she probably expected Caldwell to make his move on her again or something. When he didn't, she swallowed a bottleful of pills.''

''And I thought my family was tough to take.'' His lips were inches from hers, and she drew in a quiet breath, putting some distance between them. ''So what happens with the custody case?''

''Without Caldwell challenging my guardianship,

there is no case. You were right about him. Caldwell just wants to be a grandfather. He called the judge a few minutes ago. The kids are mine. For good.'' There was no mistaking the true relief in his expression.

''You'll be a good parent, Garrett,'' Darby said quietly.

''I'm going to try.'' His gaze was fierce on her, and she looked away.

''So you'll be going back to New Mexico soon,'' she finally said.

''Is that what you want?''

She frowned. ''That was your plan. Get G&G up and running so it could take down Castle Construction. Go back to New Mexico. All in a day's work.''

He looked around. Back to the house. ''Plans change. G&G and Castle will find a way to work together.''

''And it's all changed because of the children.''

''Yeah.'' His gaze settled on her once again. ''And you. Caldwell and I are never going to be best buds, but I'm willing to meet him partway for the sake of the kids. So why won't you marry me? We know the truth about the accident.''

Darby brushed her hands through her hair and turned around, staring sightlessly at the magnificent view. ''Because I need it all. I can't go into a marriage expecting it to end in a few years. I can't fool myself into thinking that being the children's new mother is enough for me. Not now. Not anymore.''

''Forget the prenup. We get married, we stay married. Period. You want me to say I love you. Admit it.''

She closed her eyes. Oh, Garrett. ''I want you to *feel* it,'' she corrected. But he didn't. He wouldn't let himself. She walked closer toward the waterfall, leaned her elbows on a jagged wall of outcropping rocks. She could feel the spray on her face. Or maybe that was just more tears.

"I'll tell you what I feel," he said. His voice was low, and she looked back to see him walking toward her, looking fierce and male. "You smile at me, and it makes a hell of a day suddenly go away. You laugh and push your fingers through your hair, and I find myself laughing, too. You sing to my kids, and it makes me so damn glad that they're not going to have the childhood that I did."

He took a step closer, and she could see the pulse beating in his corded throat. His voice dropped even lower as pulled her around to face him. "You make love with me, and it's like I'm not even owner of my own soul anymore, because you've taken it over and turned it into something I can't recognize. And then you turned and walked away from me, from us all, when I stupidly said you were fired, and it felt like you'd yanked my insides out with a grappling hook. I don't know if that's love. All I know is it's something I've never felt. Not for anyone." He ducked his head, pressing a hard, fast kiss to her mouth.

She tore away. "I'm a coward, Garrett! Don't you see that? I couldn't stand up to my father and insist that he let me live my own life, so I ran instead. What kind of wife would I be? What kind of mother?"

He pulled her back into his arms. "Being a coward would have meant staying in that protective cage that made you miserable. You did what you believed you had to do. That wasn't the work of a coward. You can do *anything* you put your mind to. And I think it's time we both let the past be the past. The only thing that matters is now. And what we make of the future. You're the only woman I've ever wanted as my wife. You're the only woman who can love my kids as well as you do.''

She sucked in her breath at the feel of his warmth against her. ''I don't want to make a mess of this,'' she whispered. ''I don't want to keep hurting people.''

''Then stop hurting yourself first. Stop blaming yourself for being who you are. There're five kids anxiously waiting for me to bring their Darby back home where she belongs. And there's one man who's never gonna figure out how to let his heart out of its cage if you don't take pity on him. You're our only hope, Darby.''

She looked into his eyes, those deep mossy-green eyes. And finally saw the truth. Her knees went weak, and her heart seemed so full that it might burst. ''Do we really have to go back to New Mexico?''

He smiled faintly. ''Sweetheart, I'm the boss. I can go wherever I want to go. And God help us but Caldwell has actually admitted he's wanted out of Castle for years, but responsibility kept him at it. He wants to focus on being the mayor.''

''So what are you going to do?''

''Buy him out or something. I don't know.'' He cupped her face in his hands. ''You don't want to leave Fisher Falls, do you?''

She sighed shakily. ''It's the first place I've ever really felt at home. And I...I really think that Georgie needs me, Garrett. Once she's well enough to leave the care center, I want to be here for her. She's told me time and again that she wishes her house would be filled with children's laughter. I can't imagine any better medicine for her than her living to see that become a reality.''

"What are you suggesting?'' His eyes were filled with light, as if he already knew.

She smiled at him. Loving him so much that the world really did seem suddenly full of possibilities. Thunder rolled over their heads, and a gust of wind dashed a spray of water over their heads. "Will you marry me,'' she asked, raising her voice above the noise. "Despite the family that comes with me?''

His lips slowly curved. "If you'll marry me, despite the family that comes with me.''

Laughter bubbled from her. "I can't think of anything more wonderful.''

He swept her up in his arms and carried her away from the rocks. Away from the waterfall.

"Where are we going?''

He strode steadily toward his truck. "To visit Georgie and tell her the news,'' he said. "Then I'll know that you're not going to change your mind and back out on me.''

Darby pressed her palm alongside his bristled jaw. Oh, she did love this hard, bristle-faced man. "We can tell Georgie later,'' she told him softly, surely.

"Okay. We'll go pick out a ring, then. Right now.'' He yanked open the passenger door of his truck and set her inside on the seat.

She laughed softly. "Garrett, *later.* I'm not going to change my mind about becoming your wife. I promise.''

His movements finally slowed. "What is it that you want to do then?''

She looped her hands around his neck and tugged

his head down to hers. "Take me home, Garrett. Take me home to our kids."

He kissed her, long and slow. "I never thought I'd say this, but I like the sound of that."

"So do I, my love. So do I."

Epilogue

One Month Later

"Are you ready for this?"

Darby stared out the car window as they approached the gated entrance to the Rutherford family estate in Kentucky. She pressed her lips together for a moment, then nodded. It may have taken her a month, but she *was* ready. Georgie was recuperating well and was back home. The children were happy and healthy and recovered from a brief bout with summertime colds.

There were no more reasons for Darby to put this off. It was time. And she knew it right down to her bones. "I'm ready. See that van there? The one parked across the road in the trees? Two reporters inside. Names are Fitzpatrick and Gonzales. They are always there."

Garrett closed his hand over Darby's. "Want to stop and give them a scoop?" He lifted her hand and kissed the delicate diamond ring on her finger.

She laughed softly. "Not likely."

He enjoyed the light of battle in her eyes. He slowed and turned the vehicle into the wide, curving drive, pulling to a stop next to the security guard who stepped forward from a small enclosed booth.

Darby leaned across Garrett and smiled at the guard. "Hello, Sims. Is my father or brother about today?"

"Yes, ma'am." Sims eyed her with surprise. "Shall I call ahead or—"

"We'll surprise them," Darby interrupted. "Thank you, Sims."

The guard nodded and stepped out of the way as the enormous iron gate slid open.

"Good grief," Garrett muttered as he drove the rental car through.

"I warned you," Darby murmured at his side. "There's still time to back out, you know."

"And lose out on marrying an American princess?" He grinned at her, seeing the way she rolled her eyes. He was glad to see the humorous light in her eyes again. She'd been growing increasingly tense since they'd left Minnesota early that morning.

"Do you think Caldwell and Lucinda will really be all right with the children this week? I'm not sure we should stay here in Kentucky quite as long as we'd planned."

"They're fine," Garrett assured her, though he wasn't all that delighted leaving his kids in Caldwell's care, even with Lucinda's help. Georgie's cook-cum-housekeeper had been delighted with Georgie's instructions to care for the wee ones. Not even the mayor had the nerve to disagree with Georgina Vansant. But Garrett had to admit Caldwell was making an effort, and for Darby's sake Garrett would hold up his end, too.

"Georgie…"

"…can't wait for us to get back so we can finish ironing out the details for the wedding and so she can give me more orders on work she wants done around the house," he suggested.

"You're sure you don't mind living there with her?"

He grinned at her. "She keeps things lively, that's for sure. Gives me some idea of what her great-niece will be like in another sixty years or so. She's happier than all of us combined at having her house filled with more than wind chimes and plants."

He braked and parked their rental car behind a dark-blue sports car. He looked at Darby, who was staring at the house. "You can do this," he said softly.

She looked back at him, smiling quickly. Nervously. "I suppose I shouldn't be angry with my father anymore. If I hadn't been so upset about being dismissed from my job, I wouldn't have left home. And if I hadn't done that, you and I might never have met."

Garrett brushed her lips with his. "Everything happens for a reason."

Darby rested her forehead against him for a moment. The silly jiggle in her chest had a lot more to do with the man sitting beside her than the two men she would soon face inside her childhood home. "Thanks for coming with me," she murmured.

"I faced Caldwell because of you," he murmured. "Seems only fair. But you're capable of doing this on your own. You always have been."

Darby smiled and sat back, releasing her safety belt. Garrett had such faith in her. "Not always," she corrected. "And I'm still glad you're here with me now."

She waited while Garrett rounded the car and opened her door. Then she climbed out and, holding his hand, walked up to the house and in through the front door.

Marlene, the wizened little housekeeper who'd been with the family longer than Darby had been alive, appeared from one direction and gasped. "Miss Debra! You're home."

Darby went forward, hugging the woman. "Just for a visit, Marlene," she cautioned, laughing. "But definitely long enough to have some of your Derby pie."

"Marlene?" A deep voice filled the foyer. "I could have sworn I heard— Well, holy hell. Look what the cat dragged in."

Darby looked up from Marlene into the brilliant-blue eyes of her brother. "Nice to see you, too, Dane. Sweet talk and all."

He grinned suddenly and hauled her up in his arms, swinging her around in a circle before setting her back on her feet. He looked at Garrett, then back at her. "So you're finally done hiding behind Georgie's skirts, are you?"

Darby's mouth dropped. "You...knew?"

Dane made a face. "Peanut, you can't make a move in this world without us knowing about it. Georgie denied seeing you, of course, but knowing how she and Dad argue about everything under the sun, I was still suspicious. Then I got word about Phil's accident. It seemed obvious to me even before I obtained a copy of the accident report, which included a very concise account by a witness named Darby White."

Darby reached out blindly and felt the warm security of Garrett's hand close around it. "Does Daddy know?"

Dane shook his head. "I assured him you were safe, but I managed to keep your secret. Mostly because he's been leaving the business more to me while he concentrates on another horse farm he wants to buy. You and I are a team, remember?"

Darby's eyes filled. "I remember." She blinked rapidly and turned to Garrett. "Dane, this is Garrett Cullum. My fiancé."

Dane's eyes narrowed. "Well. That *is* a surprise. How did you meet?"

"Stop looking all fierce," Darby said, suddenly amused. "Garrett, this is my know-it-all brother, Dane Rutherford." She watched the two men size each other up, apparently coming to the same decision when they stuck out their hands and shook solemnly.

"When is the wedding?"

Darby stiffened and looked up the curving staircase at the gruff question. Roth Rutherford looked the same as he'd always looked. Rich and powerful and demanding. And no matter how infuriated he could make her, she did love him.

"In three weeks," she told him clearly. "On the grounds of Georgie's place."

"I should've known not to trust that old battle-ax. She was hiding you all along."

Darby continued as if her father hadn't spoken. "And if you promise to behave yourself, we'll invite you to the wedding, and I'll let you give me away. *If* you promise."

Roth slowly descended the staircase and walked toward Darby. "If?"

She swallowed, then just said what she felt. "If you can't behave yourself, you can stay here in Kentucky, and the rest of us will enjoy the festivities. I'm not going to tolerate any more of your interference in my life, Daddy. No more trying to buy my friends or pay off those you think are my enemies. I know you believe you're only protecting me, but none of us can live that way. Not anymore."

"Are you telling me what to do?"

Her chin lifted. "Yes. I am." And it was easier than she'd ever dreamed.

His tight lips slowly eased as his gaze slid to Garrett. "I suppose *you* had something to do with Debra's newfound contrariness."

"Daddy, I'm warning you," Darby began.

"It's past time Darby was a little contrary, don't you think?" Garrett answered smoothly. "But I'm not taking credit for it. She's had it inside her all along."

Roth harrumphed. "I've already cut her off from the money. Just how much do you figure marrying my girl is worth?"

"Daddy!" Appalled Darby stepped in front of her father. "That is uncalled for."

"Fifteen million," Garrett said flatly.

Darby swayed. She looked from her father's calculating expression to Dane's curious one, and finally to Garrett's. His mossy-green gaze met hers, and she melted inside.

"Fifteen million it is," Roth said. "And then you can get the hell off my property and away from my girl."

"I don't think you understood me," Garrett said quietly. "I'm perfectly happy to leave your property, but I'm not leaving Darby." He reached inside his leather jacket and pulled out a slender checkbook. He flipped it open and began writing.

"What are you doing?" Roth blustered.

"Writing you a check for fifteen mil. That was the amount we agreed upon wasn't it?" He tore out the check and extended it toward Roth. But his eyes were on Darby. "Darby is worth more than everything I own in this world, which totals just about this amount. If you want it in exchange for a life with her, you can have it. I'm coming out on top of the deal."

Darby smiled shakily. "Oh, Garrett."

"You're plumb crazy, you know that?" Roth looked at them both. "I take that check and you two won't have anything."

"We'll have each other, Daddy," Darby cut him off.

"Each other and no money," Roth grumped.

"Each other and love," Garrett assured. He brushed his thumb along Darby's satiny cheek, not even noticing when the check drifted to the floor. "I love you. I'd love you even if it weren't for the kids."

"Kids?" Roth's voice rose. "Kids? You've haven't even been gone five months! Just what on earth have you been doing?"

Darby barely heard him. She was too entranced with Garrett. "I love you, too," she whispered.

Dane sighed noisily and leaned down to pick up the check. He tore it in half and stuck it in his pocket as he pulled his father away from the pair who seemed to have forgotten they weren't quite alone. "Close your mouth, Dad," he advised dryly. "Your girl has grown up and found herself a man as determined as you."

Roth harrumphed again. "He'd better protect her, that's all I've got to say."

Darby smiled tremulously at Garrett. They knew the truth. They would protect each other.

"Just how many *kids* are there supposed to be, anyway?" Roth's voice floated back through the foyer.

Garrett chuckled. Darby giggled. She pushed her fingers luxuriously through Garrett's dark hair and tugged his head toward hers. "He's gonna have a fit when he hears six," she murmured.

"Five," Garrett corrected.

Darby pressed her lips together and waited. It didn't take long.

"Darby?" His arms cradled her against him with such tenderness that her eyes filled with tears.

"I'm pretty sure. Do you mind?"

He slowly shook his head. "Do you?"

"I think it's perfect." Then she laughed. "It's a good thing we have plenty of bedrooms at Georgie's."

"If we didn't I'd build more myself. I meant it, Darby. Even if you and I had to start from scratch, kids and all, I'd do it."

Darby looked into his eyes and knew it was true. "Tell me again?"

Garrett's expression softened. "I love you. Not because a legend says it's so, but because I feel it." His palm settled over her flat belly. "And I promise to treasure our love for the rest of our days."

Darby covered his hand with hers. "And beyond?"

His lips met hers in a vow that nothing could ever surpass. "And beyond."

*   *   *   *   *